FEB 2009

tender
grace

tender grace

JACKINA STARK

BETHANY HOUSE PUBLISHERS
Minneapolis, Minnesota

Published by Bethany House Publishers
11400 Hampshire Avenue South
Bloomington, Minnesota 55438

Bethany House Publishers is a division of
Baker Publishing Group, Grand Rapids, Michigan.

Printed in the United States of America

Library of Congress Cataloging-in-Publication Data

Stark, Jackina.
    Tender grace / by Jackina Stark.
        p.   cm.
    ISBN 978-0-7642-0575-0 (pbk.)
    1. Widows—Fiction. 2. Conduct of life—Fiction. I. Title.
    PS3619.T3736T46   2009
    813' .6—dc22

                                                                    2008042995

For my husband, Tony

one

July 10

He died the way he'd always wanted to. As anyone would want to, I'd think—sitting in his recliner with something wonderful to read. The bad part, of course, was the juxtaposition of the numbers. He had hoped to leave the confines of the earth at age 85, not 58.

I had hoped for the same thing, hadn't thought yet to worry that he might not. His annual physical had been encouraging, as usual. No hint of heart trouble, or any other kind of trouble. He took a half tablet of Zocor and a baby aspirin only as a sensible precaution. We'd had colonoscopies on the same morning two months before he died, and we'd left the hospital congratulating ourselves on colons fit beyond our expectations.

This evening I decided to see if I could formulate words.

Except for thank-you notes, labels for Christmas presents wrapped by mall elves, and birthday cards for Mom, the kids, and grandkids, I haven't written anything since I kissed him good-night and told him to come to bed soon.

I've been sitting here in front of this new document for what seems like an hour watching the cursor of my laptop blink on and off, rhythmic as a heartbeat. The cursor seems more alive than I. Don't they say the first year is supposed to be the hardest? I'm three months into year two. Like a daffodil, the nub of it breaking through the soil in the flower beds each spring, I should be awakening.

I'm so disgusted with myself that I am not.

And I'm afraid. Afraid that this is who I am now. I read many years ago that when someone dies, there is a sense in which the loved ones die too. The optimistic twist on it was that rebirth occurs and the new person, affected by the suffering, may become better than the old. The rub lies in the auxiliary verb *may*. How I wish the "new me" were better than the old, a tribute to everything we had and were.

I assumed when the time came, that's how it would be.

I was wrong.

The truth is I know of no one who has coped worse with losing a mate than I have.

There is the small consolation that most people think I'm fine.

My children know I'm not, but they are kind and understanding and patient. But even they don't know that I feel as dead to this world as their father is. You don't tell your children that. They have suffered enough.

July 11

I record *Oprah, Law and Order, American Idol, Dancing With the Stars, Heroes, What Not to Wear, Divine Design, The Closer,* and an eclectic selection of movies, lots of movies. Next season I might add *Ugly Betty* to my schedule, despite its unfortunate title. Several people have recommended it.

No matter what my son says, I do not and will not record *American Chopper.* Is this refusal a sign of life?

My DVR holds one hundred hours of programming. I panic if the allotted time for recording reaches fifty.

Mark and Molly, caring children that they are, have encouraged me to continue substitute teaching. It's true—I did enjoy it the two years after I packed up my classroom and retired, but I have not been able to find enough interest and energy, even courage, to enter a classroom since Tom died. This strikes me as odd since I taught for thirty years, and a classroom was as much my natural habitat as water is to fish. But that was then.

Tom and I retired early, even though we still enjoyed our jobs, so that we could "run around"—that's what our friends called it. We only dabbled in running around, however. We didn't buy a travel trailer and slap a "We're spending our children's inheritance" sticker on it, but we spent a lot of time with the grandkids, and we saw a lot of the country. A cruise to Alaska was on our calendar for last July. It was our last Christmas present to each other and made us look forward even more to the new year.

We missed viewing the inner passage of Alaska by three months.

Fortunately we had insured the trip. Mother wasn't feeling well when we booked it.

July 12

I prepared for retirement by getting serious about exercise. I am not disciplined, though Molly, great defender of her mother, says I didn't get a master's degree while caring for a two-year-old and expecting another baby without discipline. Nor, she continues, did I teach for thirty years without a significant amount of discipline. I call these examples anomalies. The rule is this: little discipline.

The treadmill upstairs in the bonus room is one of my proof texts. I have exercised off and on all my life. I gain ten pounds, start dragging around, begin thinking about cutting calories and walking three miles a day, mull it over a few months, finally commit myself to it, and then lose the ten pounds and gain a level of energy that will suffice.

I always think I'll keep at it the rest of my life. Then with no warning, I quit. Eventually I gain ten pounds and the cycle begins again. When I turned fifty-two and retirement was only four months away, I told myself exercise was no longer just a good idea; it was a necessity if we were to have quality of life in what Jane Fonda calls Act Three.

The last time I was on the treadmill was the morning before Tom died, having barely finished Act Two.

July 17

Somehow I managed.

The whole crew came for a weekend visit: Mark and Katy with Kelsie and Austin; Molly and Brad with Jada and Hank—our beloveds. Could there be sweeter children and grandchildren? I remember how happy, no, *thrilled*, Tom and I were that the kids settled only an hour or so away. Branson is a little closer than Joplin, but both kids have made us feel they live just on the other side of Springfield.

We built this house on the golf course eleven years ago. I'm glad we didn't wait until we retired to do it. I had thought we might spend forty years together here. If gratitude were still a blip on my screen, I'd have to say ten years beats two.

Tom enjoyed golfing immensely, but he especially loved playing with Mark and Brad. He did not live long enough for the boys to beat him, though there was whooping and hollering the day Mark tied him. Friday evening the men took the golf cart out for the first time without Tom.

The little girls, age six now, slept with me. The little boys cried because they couldn't, but they finally settled down when Molly let them both sleep on a pallet in her room. Molly and Mark sense my weariness. Their visits have been short since Tom died, usually only overnight. So far I've been able to feign being a decent nana for twenty-four hours.

The girls will start first grade next month; I remember marveling with Tom that soon they'd be in kindergarten. How was it possible that our grandchildren were old enough for that? Nothing prepared us for the joy of our children's children. Though we adored our son and daughter and have enjoyed kids by occupation, this bliss caught us by surprise.

The "babies," as we call them, have finally quit looking for Papa when they come.

I cannot believe what they have lost. I cannot believe I'll ever be enough.

July 18

Molly and Katy had breakfast ready before the girls and I made it into the kitchen. Tom, an early riser, had been the breakfast maker when the kids came home. I got out maybe three words of apology before Molly stopped me. My new routine doesn't include breakfast, but I managed to eat part of a waffle and a piece of bacon. Sitting across from me at the round breakfast table, Molly said the flowers at the front of the house and in the beds around the patio looked gorgeous. She and Brad had come the first of May to help me put out the annuals. This was something Tom and I always did together. Molly knew I wouldn't get it done by myself.

What she doesn't know is that annuals have ceased to thrill me.

July 19

Writing the date is the answer to my blinking cursor. I can write a paragraph or two once the date gets me started. I caught sight of the last line of yesterday's entry and can't believe I said that annuals have ceased to thrill me. It seems sacrilegious and probably is. But, if I'm honest (and what a drag that is), I'd have to say many good things have ceased to thrill me.

I've quit reading, even best sellers, even Pulitzers, even the newspaper (I canceled it), even my Bible. I'm surprised I read even the last line of Tuesday's entry.

I also quit listening to music. I have chosen silence for over a year now. Molly begs for "tunes" when we're together. It's rare that I relent.

This lack of appreciation for things I once loved is beginning to define me. More mornings than I can count, I say to myself before I open my eyes, "I don't want to do this." In the days shortly following Tom's death that made sense, but what does it mean now? I asked myself that yesterday. What is "this" exactly? What does that mean?

I don't know.

That I'm in trouble?

One of the best qualities of the former me was thankfulness. In fact, on my fiftieth birthday I awoke with a doxology on my lips, aware of so many good gifts I'd received from God in fifty years, including two new grandbabies. I've even given thanks for my penchant for giving thanks. As I was trying to sleep last night, needing Tom to be curled up behind me, his left arm slung across me, nightly comfort, I realized to my horror that I couldn't remember the last time I was thankful. *Really* thankful. Not an intellectual gratitude, which has remained, but an emotional and spiritual gratitude that wells up from a trusting, peaceful heart. I thought of a line from an old hymn: "Awake, my soul, and sing."

I miss Tom.

I also miss me.

two

July 20

Our youth minister called this morning and asked if I'd teach the fourth grade for VBS next week. He asked last February, said the kids always asked for me, but I declined. "Maybe next year," I said. Fortunately finding people to help at our church isn't too difficult, and Karen Norton agreed to teach the fourth graders. Unfortunately, Grant explained, she had emergency surgery last night, leaving them "in a fix." I said I was sorry but I just couldn't do it on such short notice. I felt bad. Two summers ago they could have counted on me. I told Grant to call everyone he knew and call me back if there was literally no one else. He said there were others on his list, for me not to worry. If he calls back, I just won't answer.

It has crossed my mind that caller ID and the DVR make my life tolerable.

It was only eight when Grant called, and I was not ready to face the day. Hard as I tried, though, I couldn't go back to sleep. Finally I got out of bed, poured a Diet Coke, and sat on the back porch staring at the trees. The trees used to nourish me, but these days I merely stare at or through them.

Out of my stupor came Tom's voice, calling me to look at his tomato plants. The vines had grown above the six-foot wire contraptions he had made to encircle and protect them, and though the tomatoes were still green, they were as big around as his hand. I got out of the glider and actually walked down the steps and across to the side yard, where railroad ties outline the rectangle of his garden, empty but for soil dry and compressed after waiting so long to be cultivated.

July 21

Mom called today. She wanted to tell me "the girls" had spotted a pod of dolphins this morning. Since my dad died, she, along with five other widows in their seventies, has spent every July and August vacationing in a beach-front house in Gulf Shores. Most of them haven't missed a year in the last eight.

I asked her if she was having fun.

"We're having a blast," she said.

Then she had to go; it was her turn to deal.

July 25

Rita talked me into lunch today. She has made the transition from couple friend to solo friend. I'm sure it took some effort. The first Sunday I returned to church after Tom died, Rita dragged John to the other side of the auditorium so they could sit by me, and there they have sat every Sunday since. More often than not, when church is over, she tries to arrange something for the following week: lunch, a movie, shopping. "You'd do it for me," Rita said when I told her she does too much. It is such a relief that she never gets offended when I say, "Not this week, do you mind?" Most of my friends haven't been so tenacious. I don't blame them.

She came into the restaurant carrying a purse the size of carry-on luggage and two sacks requiring handles. When she reached our table, she looked at her sacks and laughed at herself. She had picked them up with her purse when she got out of the car. She situated them in the corner behind our table and said she and John are going on a cruise. She called it "your cruise," since Tom and I had gone on a Mediterranean cruise for our twenty-fifth anniversary.

Rita is dear to me for many reasons. That she isn't afraid to mention Tom is among them. It's one reason I sometimes accept her invitations. She and John are leaving the second week of September and will be gone almost four weeks. They're taking a land tour of Italy after the cruise. I told her Tom enjoyed that cruise but said he'd never again spend more than two weeks away from home.

Oh, but he's been gone much longer than two weeks.

And he didn't take me with him.

Four or five years ago I read about a couple in their eighties who died together in their bed, the result of a gas leak. My own grandparents died only three months apart. I have thought of these couples often . . . and envied them.

July 26

If people knew what was really going on in my life, they'd probably say I'm depressed and should get help. And I'll admit I do have some classic symptoms of depression. Still, though it takes me forever and gives me little pleasure, every day I take a shower, wash my hair, *and* put on makeup. I put on my makeup even if I plan to watch ten straight hours of recorded programming. If someone comes to the door, I might pretend I'm not home, but not because I don't look decent. I've been surprised to discover that all these years I've looked as good as possible for *myself,* not Tom, though he appreciated it. What that means, I don't know. But when I no longer care about my appearance, I'll turn myself in, and if I don't, Mark and Molly will most certainly intervene.

Music and reading are the only two things I've given up entirely. I still go to church, at least the morning worship service, I still talk with the kids and Mom, and I still invite them to come see me (but please make it brief). I still do things with Rita now and then, I play handheld games Tom used to take on planes, I keep a deck of cards nearby for solitaire, and I watch hours of television. I sometimes watch fluff stuff, but HGTV, Animal Planet, the History Channel, the Learning Channel, and the National Geographic Channel keep me enormously informed. I'm not brain dead, but I'm sure my heart is precariously close to a kind of death, because anything I do is such a chore. My life is one long sigh. That seems a crime against God's goodness to me.

That knowledge, I'm sorry to say, doesn't change anything.

July 28

I didn't pick up the phone today—not even when Molly called. I figured she'd leave a message if it were an emergency. I just didn't have the energy to sound fine. I'll call her this evening. I'll ask her what Jada and Hank have been up to and reciprocate with details about the Alaska pipeline, fresh off the History Channel.

She's lost her dad; she must not lose her mother.

July 29

I've been reading my entries. In doing so, I've realized that I have given up something besides reading and listening to music. Not quite as completely, but as significantly. I've given up speaking.

Of course I say what is necessary. And with those closest to me, I try to interact, but I've become adept at asking open-ended questions. Such questions keep others talking, and the questioner comes off as a good conversationalist. When open-ended questions need a rest, Animal Planet (et al.) comes to the rescue. There you have it: Someone who was once borderline gregarious has no desire to speak. None. I haven't even carried on an interior monologue. I've been close to comatose within.

Is that why I opened my laptop the evening of July tenth?

To speak?

July 30

I sat beside Rita in church today and felt like crying when a girl sang a song I hadn't heard in some time, since long before Tom died. The refrain is all I remember, all I heard after the first few lines: "Jesus will still be there." Not that I don't know that. "I am with you always" runs through my mind most days, even as I sigh. But as she sang I saw the image of massive hands extending from strong arms reaching over a cliff and grasping my forearms. I remained suspended in midair throughout the song, but I didn't fall.

I wouldn't have thought myself capable of such an optimistic image.

July 31

An idea came to me in the middle of the night.

Even when I was sane I tended to roll my eyes at ideas conceived under such circumstances, so I'll probably deem this one stupid too when I ponder it in the light of day.

The kids called to check on me. Today would have been our thirty-second anniversary.

A Tennyson line comes to me: "O death in life, the days that are no more."

August 1

Twenty-four hours later, the idea seems feasible. The wildness of this late-night thought trumps the desperation of my days.

I'm leaving here.

three

August 3

I've "summoned" the children. They'll come Saturday and go to church with me on Sunday. It will be nice not to go alone, nice to have friends gather around our pew to greet the kids and marvel at how cute the grandkids are.

I took the car in for an oil change and asked them to check the tires, lights, and anything else that needs checking when one is taking off on a long trip. I sat in the waiting room watching *Dr. Phil* when a man I'd never seen before started talking to me.

"Hot," he said.

I glanced away from Phil for a minute to see if the man was really talking to me. We were the only two people in the room, so I shook my head in agreement.

"It is," I said.

"A hundred three degrees."

"Whew," I replied.

"It is" and "whew" were all he needed.

He told me he laid tile for new construction, but it was just getting too hot for it; he told me about a new invention he'd come up with to take the ambiance of a tiled floor up a notch (I didn't quite follow this); he told me in detail about the design he was doing for the kitchen he was currently working on, which featured little diamond-shaped insets made of colored glass.

At some point in all this, I told him my husband laid the tile for the bathrooms in our new home.

Driving away, I thought about my conversation with Chatty Man. (Generally speaking, that might be a prize-winning oxymoron.) It struck me as interesting that I called our house *new*. Most things are relative, I suppose; nevertheless, we didn't move in last month, or last year—Tom laid those tiles *eleven* years ago.

Still, I like the present tense sound of "our new home." I can see why I chose it. I can see why I let it stand.

August 5

After we cleared the dinner table and settled the babies in the bonus room to watch *Cars* (an appropriate choice in retrospect), I asked the kids to sit with me in the living room.

"I don't mean to be mysterious," I told them, "but I'm

going on a road trip, destination and time frame undetermined."

The four of them looked at me as if I'd suggested a game of strip poker.

Molly finally said, "What do you mean?"

Then everyone was talking at once.

They began to calm down somewhat when they realized I had been carefully preparing for this trip. Even in the fog of my existence, I knew if I didn't give them an explanation of what I am planning and convince them I will be okay, they'd send the Mounties after me.

Mark was impressed that I had the car taken care of, and he was glad to hear it still had substantial warranty time left on it. Molly was relieved to see my current insurance and AAA cards filed neatly in a plastic bag, ready for the glove compartment. The size and weight of my new atlas seemed to reassure them as well.

"I may not know where I'm going from one day to the next," I said, plopping it on the ottoman in front of the sofa, "but when I decide, I'll know how to get there. Ultimately, I plan to visit an island near San Diego that your dad wanted me to see."

"That's sad, Mom," Molly said.

"Sort of, I guess. But I want to do this."

I went on to tell them that the Bennetts, who have lived across the street since we built the house, would take care of the yard and collect the mail. "Mark can pick it up once a month and pay any bills for me that aren't taken care of directly through the bank."

"Once a month!" They were a choir.

"I may be gone awhile."

My cell phone, I explained, would be on, but just for family emergencies (and to hit *55 at the first sign of trouble). I would communicate by e-mail, and I'd try to do it several times a week, at least once a week. I assured them I'd stay in nice places and be very, very careful.

When I finished, I asked if they could think of anything I'd overlooked.

"Someone to go with you," Molly said. Mark nodded in agreement.

"Who?" I asked.

The girls stared at me, eyes brimming with tears.

"I think this may be something I'm supposed to do. I won't exactly be alone, you know. Something you can think of every time you start to worry is the promise that runs through my mind almost daily: 'I am with you always.' "

Because they are children of faith, this seemed to help.

August 8

Everything is in the car except my overnight bag and this laptop. My clothes are laid out for tomorrow, a midcalf brown cotton skirt, a white tank top, and brown leather flip-flops— the usual. Tom and I always packed the car the night before a trip. He wanted an early start and nothing to impede that goal. I'm not too interested in my departure time. Whenever I get around to it. I loaded up tonight to check for things I've forgotten and to have tomorrow morning to check again.

Mark wanted me to take Tom's Tahoe, a three-row version purchased with a number of grandchildren in mind. He liked the idea of my being in something tanklike. But I'm taking my Solara. I know it well—it's my second one, and it takes much less gas. And I can park it.

Molly asked me to stop by when I told her I planned to spend the first night in Tulsa.

"Joplin's on the way, Mom," my daughter pleaded so sweetly.

I couldn't refuse her even though I will have barely been on the road an hour. The kids want to tell me good-bye again. The little boys aren't old enough to know I'm going farther than Wal-Mart, but the girls are, and they aren't much happier than their parents about this sojourn of mine. They have a charmingly limited point of view: I'm a nana, not a wanderer.

What I am is a woman who wants her old life back.

I don't know how to *be* without Tom Eaton.

August 9

Molly had a nice lunch ready for my arrival and had me on my way in an hour. She and the kids walked me to the car, gave me hugs and kisses, and waved good-bye until my car turned the corner and headed for I-44. Part of me hated leaving them.

Almost as much as I'd hated pulling out of my driveway this morning. I sat in the car with the garage door open, practically hyperventilating as I contemplated leaving everything I have loved. But in the end I put the car in reverse and drove away before the life that I have loved destroys me.

Getting my overnight bag, two suitcases, and this laptop into my room (upstairs and down two hallways) took so much energy that I may stay here a week instead of two days. If that's the case, I could have saved a good deal of money by staying at Mom's, but I simply wasn't up for going there without Tom. My room here has a microwave and a refrigerator, and I picked up a Weight Watchers meal for dinner. I also purchased a twelve-pack carton of Diet Coke and hope it will last until morning.

One of these days, I may stay at a hotel and use room service. I did that once when Tom took me with him to a principals' conference in Orlando. I rather liked it. I really don't mind eating alone, but I don't want to eat alone in public. Who cares, I'm sure. But "know thyself," and I'm just not up to that.

My plan is to run down to the complimentary breakfast room tomorrow, should I wake up before breakfast is cleared away, and get a pastry and three pieces of fruit, two of them for my lunch. I've never done that before, but Rita does it all the time. I hope an alarm doesn't go off when I walk through the doors with contraband fruit stashed in my purse.

I saw Tom's Bible sitting in the passenger seat when I was unloading the car. I put it there this morning after I made one last walk through the house and noticed it resting on the table by Tom's chair, neglected for such a long time now. In the last fifteen months I've picked it up only on the rare occasions I've been compelled to dust the table it was sitting on. The morning I found Tom, that black leather Bible, worn from years of study, was in his lap, open to John 4 in preparation for a lesson he expected to teach the next Sunday. I had opened the door to the garage before I decided to go back and retrieve it. That Bible is the only thing of Tom's I brought with me.

That—and what's left of my heart.

It's eight thirty and still pretty light outside. I went over and pulled the curtains, and now it's as black as a moonless midnight in here. And it's quiet, very quiet. I like that.

It's been a long day. This is the first motel room I've checked into by myself. I stood at the counter while the clerk processed my credit card and prepared my key envelope and felt like I was having an out-of-body experience. Yet while this all seems very strange, I think I can sleep. Sleeping is one of my gifts. I'm consistently among the twenty-six percent of Americans who get enough sleep at night. But if I'm wide awake when *Law and Order* is over, I'll take the Excedrin PM I brought along for emergencies.

I ran into a problem on the drive to Tulsa today. I'm surprised the potential for it eluded me while I planned.

The problem? Hours to think. I about panicked. My diversion was gone: You cannot watch television while driving. But then I remembered I have satellite radio with two or three thousand talk radio channels. I've paid for it all these months without using it.

Before I turned on the radio, I had been thinking about the time Tom and I visited Mom and Dad in Broken Arrow and went into Tulsa to spend an afternoon walking through the galleries of the Gilcrease Museum. There was a sculpture there that very nearly mesmerized me. Each time Tom and I became separated, he found me standing in front of it.

"It's captivating, don't you think, Tom?" I said the first time he found me there. It became our designated meeting place.

I've laid out clothes for tomorrow, even ironed the skirt. I changed it up a bit—white skirt, brown sweater set, and brown slides. I don't want to flip-flop or freeze my way through the museum. I've stayed an extra day in Tulsa to find my bronze sculpture and see if it's as lovely as I remember.

August 10

I made it to the museum by eleven. For me, that was pretty good.

I picked out a painting for Tom: *Morning in Aspen Grove*.

He would have loved it, and I would have spent as much time as he would allow searching through prints trying to find it for him.

I found a painting for me too: Homer's *Watching the Breakers*. Two women stand at the edge of the sea watching the waves break on the boulders near their feet. It instantly reminded me of another Tennyson poem, "Break, Break, Break."

Like "Tears, Idle Tears," with its haunting last line, "O death in life, the days that are no more," this poem also speaks of the helpless misery of loss. In college I couldn't fathom the kind of anguish his words suggest. But in the first month or two after Tom's death, before I declared a complete moratorium on reading, I pulled my English literature anthology off a shelf and let Tennyson's lines speak for me:

> *But O for the touch of a vanished hand,*
> *And the sound of a voice that is still!*

How easy Tennyson is to memorize:

> *Break, break, break,*
> *At the foot of the crags, O Sea!*
> *But the tender grace of a day that is dead*
> *Will never come back to me.*

I spent quite some time with the Homer painting. I left it finally to take a lunch break, rummaging in my purse for an apple while I searched for a private bench where I could hide out and stare into space.

I looked for the sculpture everywhere I went this afternoon

and thought I'd surely find it in the Native American room. When I didn't, I was so disappointed that I did something very unlike me, at least at this point in my life: I asked about it. I was so pleased when the lady said they still had it and directed me to the library reading room.

And there he stood, just as I remembered him.

He is a young Indian, exuding dignity. His hair in simple braids, he wears what appears to be buckskin pants with some kind of loincloth over them. He is looking up, and his arms are outstretched beside him, palms up. The work of artist Charles H. Humphriss, the sculpture is called *Appeal to the Great Spirit*.

Like before, I did not want to leave.

Unlike before, I felt suffocated by the desire for Tom to meet me there.

four

August 11

I took my sweet time getting around this morning before I left for Oklahoma City. I knew I didn't have far to drive, hardly two hours, so I didn't remove the *Privacy Please* sign on the door of my room until checkout time forced me to leave at noon.

Just before ten I had gone down to the breakfast room and grabbed breakfast and lunch. When I had eaten my pastry and tidied the room, I plopped myself on the plump comforter, settled myself into the bevy of pillows propped against the headboard, and reached for the remote. In my peripheral vision, however, I saw Tom's Bible sitting next to my suitcase.

When had I brought it in?

I don't know why I've refused to read even the Bible for

so long. Or why this morning I still hesitated, why I had to say to myself, "*Do* this."

After such a hiatus, what to read?

I thought about opening it and reading whatever my finger landed on. People do that, you know. But instead I opened to the place Tom had marked with the card I gave him on our twenty-fifth anniversary, the first chapter of John. He had been taking our small group through John on Sunday nights. I settled back, thinking I'd read a chapter. A few verses into it I realized that a chapter was way too much for this shrunken spirit of mine. I ended up reading only a few of the verses Tom had highlighted in chapter one.

In them Jesus is called *life* and *light*.

Maybe I should begin calling him those things, my antithesis: dear Life, dear Light.

I usually call God my *Father*, because as these verses say, I am a "child of God." I have not forgotten that. My lostness is emotional, not spiritual. It is my earthbound existence that is in jeopardy. There are spiritual implications, of course. My choosing "death in life," however unwittingly, seems worse than ingratitude; it seems a betrayal of Life and Light.

And I wonder, *Will he come to the likes of me?*

The answer comes to me, an echo of the words I offered the kids mere days ago: *"I am with you always."*

I needed a Coke break, which required an ice run. While ice tumbled into my little plastic bucket, I thought about another verse I read this morning: "From the fullness of his grace we have all received one blessing after another."

My bronze Indian gets that.

I wish I did. When you're emotionally dead, you don't see. You don't want. You don't need. You don't care. I wish I could see and embrace and rejoice in the blessings instead of hating this post-Tom existence.

Post-Tom!

Delete that compound modifier! It appalls me. It irritates me. It grieves me.

"Class, *post-Tom* is just the sort of modifier we want to cut from our papers," I'd say, ambling down two rows of desks. "*Ruthlessly* cut," I'd add with a two-handed machete move.

(Teaching high school language arts has contributed to my madness.)

But how dishonest it would be to malign those two words. They're perfectly good descriptive words. If I'm going to grieve a word, perhaps it should be the word *hating*.

⌒

I found a *Law and Order* episode to watch before I got on the Internet and started planning tomorrow. The one thing I'm sure I won't be doing is the zoo. I've been to one too many zoos in the last five years. Three summers ago, Tom and I were horrified at a bear's behavior when we visited him in his very nice habitat. With gasps (actually I gasped,

Tom laughed) we turned the boys' strollers toward the big cat section and called the little girls away from the iron fence enclosing the uninhibited grizzly. "Hurry, girls," we said, "the tigers want to see you!"

As zoos go, few could beat the St. Louis Zoo anyway, the bear notwithstanding. There is a botanical garden here I might visit. I've always considered botanical gardens quite enjoyable. They used to have the power to both enchant and calm me. There's a modern art museum as well. I could try to stretch myself and embrace modern art, instead of sitting insatiably before Renoirs and Monets. Maybe another time.

If Tom were here, we might take in the National Softball Hall of Fame. He had loved going to Cooperstown to visit the Baseball Hall of Fame. New York was our destination for our thirtieth anniversary, our last anniversary. We had a week in the city and a week in the countryside, together with our friends John and Rita, the trip culminating with Niagara Falls. We didn't mean, we had told each other, to plan anything so obviously romantic. We weren't the type. But the falls were phenomenal, like all such places, beyond what any picture or painting can express. Rita apparently does not believe this. It was she, leaning too far over a rail to get a better picture of this natural wonder than any postcard has rendered, who took the edge off romantic. And John too. Shocked by her uncharacteristic daring, and probably frightened as well, he called her stupid. Of course, we all knew he didn't mean it.

Actually, I might have sent my husband off to see the

Softball Hall of Fame by himself. "Let's meet at such and such restaurant on the river walk for lunch," I'd say, confident there would always be a later when we could be together.

I'm going to the memorial tomorrow. I'll see what seems good after that.

August 12

Tom always drove on any trips we took, short or long. The only exception was when he decided to drive home nonstop from Southern California, a destination that had been both conference and vacation. He admitted he needed a few hours' sleep when we hit Albuquerque and agreed to let me take over for six hours. I told him that navigating from Southern California to Springfield is not rocket science: There's I-40 and there's I-44. You'd have to work at getting lost. Somehow he relaxed enough to sleep, and he awoke refreshed, eager to take back the wheel and get us to Springfield. When I unfolded myself out of the passenger seat at the end of the twenty-five-hour marathon, I told him I hoped he enjoyed that little challenge, because I planned never again to ride in a car more than ten hours on any one day, preferably eight.

Surely there are roses to smell, Tom!

In fairness, he was destination oriented. He'd smell the roses when we got where we were going. And the truth is, I liked the passenger seat, reading and dozing to my heart's content. I would love to have that luxury again, at least the dozing part. But I have discovered that I can stay awake and both drive and navigate.

How freaked Tom would be to learn I went only from Tulsa to Oklahoma City before stopping. He saw nothing in Oklahoma City on any trip we made in that direction, except possibly a convenience store. In his opinion we would have just gotten on the road.

So I had not seen the Oklahoma City Memorial until today. It ended up being my only destination. I slept late, watched a movie, and e-mailed the kids, so I didn't arrive until late afternoon. As it turned out, that was good, because when I had been there awhile, I knew I had to stay until dark.

I really had no idea what to expect. When Rita's son got married last year, one wedding and reception I *had* to attend, Rita put me at a table with two couples I knew from church and with some old friends of hers from Oklahoma City. I tried to be friendly to the couple none of us knew and pulled up all my reserves to ask one of my open-ended questions.

"So," I had asked the man whose name I've forgotten, "is the memorial nice?"

"I guess," he said.

Then he looked at me as if I had no education, formal or otherwise, and added, "It's a *memorial*!"

Well, okay then.

I flashed him a quick little smile instead of thanking him for the patronizingly obvious and returned to my chicken and steamed vegetables. The other two couples could make Rita's friends feel comfortable. It was beyond me. At least he was.

I'll admit it wasn't the most astute question, but had he been anything but a Neanderthal, he could have said something like, "It's *much* more than nice. You really must see it."

I'm glad I did. The three-acre site is a stunning symbolic tribute to everyone involved in the horrific 1995 bombing. I now know why a committee could unanimously agree on one design out of 624 entries.

I wanted to stay at the memorial until the lights came on to illuminate the Survivor Tree and the glass pedestals the granite chairs rest on, revealing the names of those who died.

While I waited, a lady around my age arrived and sat down nearby. I looked over at her just as she looked at me. I almost turned away; instead I spoke, shocking myself and maybe her.

"They've built something beautiful in this horrid place," I said.

She nodded and smiled. I thought she'd look away and sit in peace as I had intended to do, but she pointed at one of the memorial chairs. "My daughter," she said.

Amazingly enough, I kept eye contact, but I didn't say anything. I had no adequate response. She seemed to see that in my eyes.

August 13

I slept so late I almost missed church. Fortunately I had located one on my way to the memorial yesterday, so I knew my way, knew the service started at eleven. I sat in the back row and was out of there with the *amen* of the benediction; nevertheless, I had met with others to worship. That seemed like a good and very responsible way to spend part of my morning.

For lunch I picked up a hamburger and malt and took this fine meal back to the hotel. After I finished eating, I chewed two antacid tablets (small price to pay for grease and chocolate) and thought about taking myself to the botanical garden. But Sunday is the designated day of rest, so I decided to take a nap instead. A long one. Evidently yesterday wore me out.

My encounter with the lady sitting near me by the Survivor Tree may have contributed to my weariness, which was more a heaviness of the heart. She said she comes to the memorial once a month or so. The year it opened she came every week. She was overwhelmed the first time she saw her daughter's name glowing in the glass base of her granite chair.

"I've wondered if I should quit coming so often," she said. "But once a month isn't too much, is it?"

It has been over a decade since her daughter died. Perhaps her question was rhetorical, but I answered her anyway.

"No," I said, "it doesn't seem too much, not to me."

We sat and looked toward the chairs for a while before I

asked, "Has being here given you the gifts mentioned in the inscription over the gates?"

"Comfort?" she asked. "And strength and peace and hope and serenity?"

She knew the inscription well. I smiled a yes.

"Yes and no," she said. "I think such gifts come from above, but this is a wonderful place for God to do his work in me. And being here helps remind me that in this world we all suffer, sometimes horribly, and yet he will help us survive. Even thrive."

She asked me if I had lost someone.

"Not in the bombing," I said.

We parted then. We hugged each other, of all things, and walked away without another word.

August 14

I have spent one more day in Oklahoma City. I made it to the botanical garden. For someone who has been eschewing annuals, I found myself halfway enjoying the flowers, plants, bushes, and ponds. At one point, I actually wished I had brought a camera, thinking the scope of a stunning flower or landscaped pond, unlike a Niagara Falls or Grand Canyon, possible to capture.

I wish I'd had a camera for my Indian brave and for the Survivor Tree too.

But it comes to me that these entries are my record, as

surely as photographs. And this choice of record has accomplished something besides recollection: Inside my head at least, I find I can speak.

This morning Tom's Bible sat on the table next to my shoe bag, staring at me. "Oh, okay," I said, picking it up. The anniversary card still marked chapter one of John, and I read his highlighted verses near the end of the chapter. Jesus invites interested disciples to come and see what he's about, and they take him up on it.

I used to be among those eager to "see." Or at least willing. Listlessness, however, has robbed me of inquiry and openness. But I sat there this morning, holding the Word of God, and wondered if a willingness to see might once again define me.

five

August 15

When I looked in the rearview mirror and saw flashing lights, what I wanted more than anything in this world was for me and my Solara to materialize in my garage. I pulled the car over, and while people with somewhere to go zoomed by me, I closed my eyes and whispered, "I want to go home."

Apparently I had forgotten to reset the cruise. If I don't set the thing, I can drive ninety miles an hour without even knowing it. The first time Tom and I bought a car with cruise control, he showed me how to use it before we left the dealership. "This little feature is going to save us some money, Audrey." I had smiled at the plural pronoun. *We* did not accumulate tickets—I did, the one I received on my fortieth birthday the most notable. Yet with each ticket, Tom, forever supportive, always pointed out I never had enough in any two-year period to lose my license.

The officer, younger than Mark, took all my information and informed me I was going twelve miles over the speed limit.

Only twelve?

"Where are you going in such a hurry, Mrs. Eaton?"

Funny he should ask.

I told him Dallas was my likely destination and I was sorry I wasn't paying close enough attention to the speedometer.

He looked like a no-nonsense, black-and-white kind of guy, so I was astounded when he said he'd let me go with a warning this time. After he handed me my driver's license and insurance card, he said, "Slow it down now, ma'am, and enjoy your visit to Texas."

"Thanks," I said, unable to look up and make eye contact with him to underscore my appreciation.

I could have been home in eight hours, but his advice, nothing more than a pleasantry really, was sign enough to keep me from turning the car around.

Texas. Enjoy.

So, here I am in Dallas, in a very nice hotel. I actually used valet parking. This I cannot easily do. Tom's frugality has rubbed off on me. I tell myself I'm using our Alaska cruise refund for this little journey. Myself replies, "And then some."

I rode the trolley today just to get a feel for at least part of the city. Tom and I took some kind of city tour almost everywhere we went and learned things we would never have known otherwise. We especially loved the boat tour around New York City and the bus tour through Rome. As I bought my ticket and found my seat on the trolley, I wondered if it would depress me to do this without Tom. But though I seemed to be the only person alone during the long ride, I was okay. No one made me scrounge up an open-ended question, no one implored me to teach VBS, no one suggested I join a water aerobics class or take up Pilates. I enjoyed passively sitting there watching people enjoying each other, or in a few cases, not enjoying each other. People, for the most part, have an agenda when riding a trolley. No one paid the slightest attention to me, except for a little boy, maybe three or four, who kept looking around his mom to smile at me. I had to smile back. He reminded me of my little boys waiting for me in Missouri.

I got off the trolley at a couple of places, but I didn't really linger anywhere. Instead I came back to my room, ordered room service, and watched a movie. I felt I deserved it after a four-hour drive, a run-in with an officer of the law, and the stretch of taking a trolley tour without Tom next to me, our tickets tucked safely in one of his pockets.

I have to get online and see what I can do here in the next day or two, should I decide to leave my room. Tom would never have come to Dallas if the Cowboys weren't playing. The Saturday I told the kids about this trip, the boys watched Cowboy quarterback Troy Aikman as he was inducted into the NFL Hall of Fame. That was another one of those times I walked through the living room and thought, *Where's Tom?*

Don't go there, Audrey.

God has been good to me today. He's always good to me. What did John 1:16 say? We have received one blessing after another?

Tom and I had so much. Why can't I get over wishing we had more?

No one has to tell me how greedy that is.

August 16

My hotel room is near Dealey Plaza, where John Kennedy was assassinated, a short walk to the Sixth Floor Museum. While I found the museum interesting enough, I was more moved simply walking along the street where the motorcade passed, where President Kennedy was hit, where Jackie cradled her husband's shockingly wounded head in her arms. I've always thought it ironic that I was sitting in a dreary classroom taking an American History test when tragedy struck the Kennedy family November 22, 1963, but it was on this sun-drenched afternoon almost a half century later that I closed my eyes against the terror and sorrow they must have felt.

I needed a television fix and turned toward the hotel.

On my way back to the safety of my room, however, I changed my mind, deciding I could manage a walk in a nice shopping district nearby. I haven't window-shopped in a long time, not even when Rita asked. Actually, I have never been all that interested in window-shopping. Tom was one husband who never had occasion to say that his wife "shopped till she dropped." I know what I need and enter a mall focused on my mission. But once my focus shifted from the past to the present, I practically strolled along the street, sipping a Diet Coke, stopping here and there to look at window displays.

One display actually did its job. It drew me into the store to replace my abominable canvas tote purse with the camel leather bag in the window. Since this bag sat in the window on a pedestal by itself, always a sign to keep walking, I figured the canvas tote and I would spend a little more time together. Still, I threw away my empty cup, walked inside, and quickly found the purse on a shelf, a twenty-percent-off sign on an easel beside it. I can't say the price was reasonable, but it was manageable.

I almost changed my mind about buying it when I realized the shortest line to a cash register had four people in it. I still can't believe I joined the line. But that choice led to more strangeness.

I began to notice that the ladies in line in front of me were agitated. The clerk behind the cash register, curt to the point of rude, proved to be the reason. On rare occasions, I've walked into a store where a clerk has been ridiculously snooty. I've always been tempted to say, "Is it my imagination or do you have to work for a living?" But until today I've never encountered an *angry* clerk, not noticeably angry anyway.

She snatched the items from the first customer, handled the transaction, and sent her off without a *Thank you*, a *Have a nice day*, or a *Please come back*. The next lady had a return, and without a word the clerk rolled her eyes and pointed to the customer service desk in the back. The poor customer didn't even know what she meant; the lady behind her explained what she needed to do. The third lady, who had been so helpful to Customer Number Two, left the line to find another line, which left only the lady in front of me. She told the clerk the sweater set she handed her was on sale, and the clerk informed her that no, it was not. When she scanned it and confirmed that it was indeed full price, Customer Number Four threw the two pieces at her and told her to keep them.

This wasn't Dante's fifth circle of hell, but it was close.

And it was my turn. After the clerk picked the sweaters off the floor and tossed them into a bin, she looked at me as if to say, *What do* you *want?*

Excuse me? Does anyone here need this?

I felt like jumping over the counter and choking her. A sense of decorum and fear of arrest kept me from following through with that tempting idea.

"Never mind," I said, making it clear how weary she had made me. I turned from the accessories counter and took the purse back to the shelf where I had found it, leaving Satan's little helper to torment Customer Six.

I feel bad about the lady now. I would guess her bad day began long before she arrived at work. I should have given her a break instead of being so very superior. I think it's safe to say she didn't mistake me for one of God's blessings today. Right back at you, I could say, but that doesn't help. Not in the least.

August 17

I've crashed. I'm staying right here today.

If I'm going to relax in a room, this is a good one to do it in. There's a nice desk with an Internet hookup, a comfortable oversized chair and ottoman, and a great television that can be viewed from the bed or the chair. I won't think about the fact that my room at home is just as nice and costs nothing. Tom made our last mortgage payment the May before he died. We took our trip to New York to celebrate that feat almost as much as our thirtieth anniversary. Our payments had been relatively low because of the down payment from the equity on our previous homes and because of money Tom's dad left him, but it was nice to have the house free and clear. And here I sit, paying "rent" today.

I won't go home until it ceases to be a tomb.

I e-mailed the kids. I told them to tell the babies that the little boy on the trolley made me miss them. Molly says everyone hopes I'm home by September. I told her we'd see how it goes.

Before I left, I notified most of the people in my address book that I was going to be gone for a month or so. I didn't say I was taking my laptop with me, though a few friends will probably assume it. Still, my in-box has been empty except for notes from the kids and one from Rita. Messages had diminished greatly in the last year anyway, because I so seldom looked at or answered my e-mail. Forwards had about come to a complete halt. That, I must say, was a relief. Mom doesn't e-mail, because she doesn't have or want a computer; she won't even let me use the word *mouse* around her unless it's the kind that leaves droppings. I called her before I left and gave her a version of my plans and said I'd call when I got home. She told me to have a good time on my "little adventure." Molly said she'll check on her and keep us posted on each other. The last I heard, Mom and her buddies were dreading leaving the beach house at the end of August.

I've watched a lot of television today too, but I haven't come close yet to the ten-hour average of the last fifteen months. I made myself turn it off this afternoon and read something from John today. Why good, simple, enjoyable things have become so difficult, I do not know.

I could have guessed Tom would have highlighted John 3:16, but he also highlighted 3:17 and wrote "Yes!" in the margin: "God did not send his Son into the world to condemn the world, but to save the world through him."

I know this is a salvation passage, the gospel encapsulated. So I hope God doesn't mind that I applied it to my current emotional state. It occurred to me as I read these verses that God probably isn't condemning me for how badly I've handled things. Satan is the accuser. God is in the saving business.

Did he put Tom's Bible in front of me and insist I bring it along? Has he eased me into situations where I must engage life outside the walls of the home Tom and I built with such love?

I *have* noticed one thing: Since I left home I haven't once awakened with the thought, *I don't want to do this.* I may not be moving very fast or doing very much, but I'm doing more than watching ten hours of television a day. I'm a long way from holding a glass half full, or even half empty, but I think I've peeked into the cabinet where the glasses are kept.

In the spirit of that much enthusiasm, I've decided to take myself to the theater tonight to see *South Pacific.* That's extreme—so extreme my heart races thinking about it.

six

August 18

Tom and I never got farther south in Texas than Dallas.

I decided to visit San Antonio because I've never seen the Alamo. I pulled up to the Hyatt (the zenith of my splurging) a little after six, surprised at how eager I was to see the old mission. Even though I surrendered my coonskin cap and overcame my Davy Crockett obsession by the fifth grade, the story of the patriots who gave their lives to fight against Santa Anna's tyranny continues to fascinate me.

I admire their courage. I wish some of it would be lurking in the air, just waiting for me to absorb it.

When I think of San Antonio, I also think of the River Walk. Even Branson has a river walk now, but I heard of this one long before I heard of any others. I can see it from my eighth-floor window. I wish Tom could see it. We would have had fun exploring this place. I considered not coming to San Antonio. I have dreaded going where he hasn't gone or seeing what he hasn't seen.

But somehow here I am.

And I got a room, which, as it turns out, was a coup. There's a canoe race tomorrow, and this place is bustling. The friendly bellman, who doesn't look a day over twenty, told me all about it on the way up. He rattled off groups and organizations that would be racing, including the Boy Scouts and Girl Scouts. He said I could watch from my room if I wanted.

His friendliness demanded some comment. What to say?

"I'll stand up here and root for the Girl Scouts."

He congratulated me on getting this room at the last minute, a choice room at that. He apparently had been nearby when the assistant manager told me someone had just canceled.

"Unfortunate for them," I told the young man, "fortunate for me."

I tried to make up for my lack of interesting banter with a good tip. He smiled, and I was glad I had at least attempted conversation.

I may indeed watch the race from my room tomorrow. I doubt I'll venture into the bedlam. I did get out for a while this evening, though. Since it was still light after I settled in my room, I rushed over to the Alamo only to find it was already closed. I rattled the doors in my frustration. If I'd had a pole, I would have vaulted myself over the walls. Actually, they're low enough that I might have been able to scamper over them—were I the scampering type. I was disappointed I couldn't see inside tonight. The outside itself, however, was a sight to behold, once I got over the shock of the diminutive edifice sitting right in the middle of this city. I am a victim of cinema and history books filled with period pictures. I expected miles of dusty plains to surround it, not glass and concrete and a smattering of grass.

I walked back to the hotel, ordered room service, and e-mailed the kids that I had arrived safely at my next destination. I didn't mention my run-in with the highway patrol, but I told them about wanting to pole-vault over the walls of the Alamo and about going to the theater in Dallas last night. I'm not sure they'll know what to think about the latter.

Even I don't know what to think. I have never gone to a play, or even a movie, by myself. Nor have I gone out at night by myself since Tom's death. I can't say I was all that eager to see *South Pacific*, but Carrie Underwood wasn't in town. Besides, can the people who have flocked to it for over fifty years be that wrong? In my experience, even one song can save a musical, and I thought "Some Enchanted Evening" had the potential for making my effort worth it. "I'm Gonna Wash That Man Right Outta My Hair," memorable as that one line is, certainly wouldn't have pried me from my hotel room.

I wore my sleeveless black dress with a V-neck in both the front and the back. Tom loved that dress. I bought it for his retirement reception. The diamond drop necklace he gave me in New York on our thirtieth anniversary looks especially beautiful with it. My hair, almost shoulder length now, is long enough to pull up in a loose updo, and I took extra care with my makeup, though as Tom often pointed out, I spend an awful lot of time on my eye makeup just to have my eyes hidden behind bangs.

"They're wispy," I'd say.

"They're long," he'd say, brushing them out of my eyes.

He wasn't here to brush them aside tonight, so I fluffed my own bangs out of my eyes and walked to the elevator carrying my sequined black clutch purse and feeling a confidence I did not expect under such circumstances. No one was in the elevator except for a man about Tom's age, dressed more elegantly than I. When I walked through the doors and gave him a fleeting look, he smiled, and I returned my standard smile for such encounters, quick and polite. When we stopped at the fifth floor, for what turned out to be an empty hallway, I realized he was staring at me.

Was my zipper undone?

I had no zipper.

Did I have lipstick on my teeth?

Who would know? My teeth hadn't made an appearance since I got on the elevator.

What?

Perhaps he merely appreciated my posture. I've been popping calcium pills since my middle thirties, and my bones seem to be thriving.

Whatever the reason for the scrutiny, the minute we reached the first floor, I rushed out of the elevator and *click, click, click*ed my way across the lobby in my black heels, through doors opened for me, and into a waiting cab, even though I had fully intended to get directions and drive.

I slid across the black leather seat and told the driver the name of the theater. I didn't bother telling him I might be coming right back since I would be arriving without a ticket.

Tom always took care of that. But I remembered our going to a concert at the last minute one time and finding two wonderful seats still available, and I thought it could happen again, especially since I needed only one. And as it turned out, a perfect seat was available—row ten, right in the middle of the auditorium.

Tom and I have had our share of perfect seats at plays and concerts. And some that weren't so perfect. We were behind a pole at a Josh Groban concert, and we were so far away from the stage at a Garth Brooks extravaganza we had to use binoculars. But we had box seats at *The Phantom of the Opera* in Chicago and center orchestra seats when we saw Richard Harris in *Camelot*.

Tom liked *Camelot*, but I loved it. Richard Harris's performance thrilled me. They have stayed with me, his last three words after King Arthur's kingdom was destroyed and the experiment of the Round Table had failed. A young boy found him in the rubble of the countryside and told the king that he wanted to be a knight of the Round Table. This moment was

Arthur's pinpoint of light in his darkest night. As I recall, he had the boy kneel so that he could knight him. Then he sent him away from the hostilities, shouting, "Run, boy, run!"

I feel some affinity with the boy's desire for something worthwhile and Arthur's hope for the return of a glorious day.

We had good seats when we saw Celine Dion too. I had wished we were in the privacy of our hotel room when she sang so passionately the song that we had replayed so many times we thought of it as "our song."

"I'm your lady," she sang, "and you are my man."

I leaned my head against Tom's shoulder as Celine sang about heading for something she didn't understand, frightened but ready to learn "the power of love."

That is most definitely how I felt when I met Tom Eaton the fall of my twenty-second year. He was the first man I had been willing to date in two years, and while I might have been afraid, he most certainly wasn't.

⌒

I guess I'd have to say I enjoyed *South Pacific* even though I had no choice but to return to the hotel the way I had come.

I've had an irrational fear of cab drivers since the day in sixth grade when Mom's car wouldn't start and I had to take a taxi to my piano lesson one freezing afternoon in January. The driver who brought me to the theater, friendlier than an insurance salesman, made a dent in my residual hesitation.

I knew the names of his three kids before we pulled up in front of the marquee and I had to fork over enough money for his older son's braces.

The cab driver who took me back to the hotel, however, had nothing to say other than, "Where to?"

Thus, with the lights of Dallas as a backdrop, I became lost in thoughts of the musicals Tom and I had seen together, lost in the songs that had made them so memorable: "Sunrise, Sunset" from *Fiddler on the Roof,* "Climb Every Mountain" from *The Sound of Music,* "Memory" from *Cats,* "All I Ask of You" from *The Phantom of the Opera*. Such beautiful music we loved.

Then I thought of one of the songs from *Camelot,* one I doubt Tom would have remembered. It began to dominate my thoughts, to play in my mind as richly as if I sat before an orchestra accompanying Celine or one of the great Italian tenors. It played as I rode through the streets of Dallas, as I took the elevator to my room, and as I hung up my dress and took off my makeup. It was still playing when I mercifully fell asleep.

"No, no, not in springtime, summer, winter, or fall. No, never could I leave you, at all."

August 19

This afternoon I braved the crowds and got my first look inside the Alamo. Despite the pathos the place evokes, I wanted to absorb it. I stood trying to imagine men and boys fighting to the death so that someday Texas would be victorious, and I tried to imagine women with their children, huddled in the corner of a room, fearing and dreading the cost of future freedom.

When I finished my self-guided tour, I walked over to get a pizza and sat at a booth, working hard to look like someone waiting for a carry-out order instead of someone sitting in a booth by herself. The difference, for a reason I can't explain, matters. Clearly, any courage that may have been left in the Alamo didn't come across the street with me.

Twenty minutes later I walked into the impressive lobby of the Hyatt and felt somewhat conspicuous, wearing crop jeans and a tank top and carrying a box containing a small pizza, thin-crust beef with extra cheese.

I am glad I saw the Alamo, but I am also glad to be back in my room.

It is remarkable that I left the room at all today. Besides watching television from my bed and the canoe races from my window this morning, I opened Tom's Bible to John 4 and found notes tucked in the pages. When I unfolded them and saw Tom's neat handwriting, a blend of printing and cursive, I drew in my breath.

Quite unexpectedly, I was taken to a place I've been avoiding for so long. I woke up that early morning aware that Tom's side of the bed was empty. The lighted digital numbers on the clock radio said 3:15. I hated sleeping without him and was surprised I hadn't awakened sooner. I got up and went to the bathroom and then started for the living room, where I assumed Tom had fallen asleep, like he did a good many nights, watching a ball game or reading a book.

"Tom," I called as I came out of our bedroom and into the living room. He was sitting in the recliner, just as I had suspected.

But immediately, I knew everything had changed. I could tell by looking at him in the soft lamplight that he had left his mortal body behind to put on an immortality that I am not yet privileged to see. I stood across the room from him and shut my eyes, hoping it wasn't true.

"Not yet," I whispered.

But I knew our time together was over. I walked over to him, placed my palm on his cold face, kissed the corner of his mouth, folded his notes, and closed his Bible and placed it on the ottoman. Then, before I phoned 9-1-1 and before I made the wretched calls to the children, I backed away from Tom, looking at his beautiful, peaceful face, and dropped into my overstuffed chair across the room.

Three short words reminiscent of a line from a Frost poem came to me: *All is ruined.*

⌒

I have not cried since I found Tom that morning. I have felt numb, and I have preferred it that way. Or maybe instead of insensibility it is a case of Wordsworth's "thoughts that . . . lie too deep for tears."

I never had trouble crying before he died; it was not

difficult to touch or even break my heart. Tom said my sensitivity was one of the qualities that drew him to me. He said he was too objective, too black and white, too businesslike. He said I was his complement. He would be so surprised to hear me talk of insensibility, listlessness, stupor. I think he'd be glad I am making this journey.

I scoured his notes looking for anything remotely personal, but all I found was a lesson outline on the first section of John 4, where Jesus speaks with the woman at the well, a woman who might have been miserable enough to take off like I have if she could have managed such a thing. Tom listed three things their encounter tells us about God and his people: (1) he knows everything about us, (2) he still wants relationship with us, and (3) he offers us what no one else has to give, living water. Jesus says this water is like a "spring of water welling up to eternal life." Tom's notes say he's offering "vigorous, abundant life." That is a strange group of words, as mysterious to me these days as hieroglyphics.

If I were sitting on the edge of Jacob's well, looking into the eyes of Life himself, would I believe that all is not ruined, that something so glorious as abundant life is possible? Can I muster up enough wisdom and trust and courage to accept his offer of living water?

I thought of something this morning as I sat holding Tom's Bible, trying to recover from thoughts of finding Tom that April morning. The fourth of April, two days before Tom died, we spent the afternoon working in the yard. That night, invigorated by a day of spring sunshine and manual labor, we made love, candlelight flickering on the golden yellow walls. Afterward, instead of falling quickly into a relaxed sleep, we talked for at least a half hour about the kids, about what we wanted to do to the yard that spring, about the upcoming trip to Alaska. We talked until Tom began drifting off.

I raised myself up on my elbow, leaned over, and kissed him lightly on his soft, warm lips.

"I love you, Tom Eaton," I said.

He opened his eyes, smiled sleepily at me, and closed them again. Then as I rolled over and snuggled into my side of the bed, I heard him mumble, "I love you too, Audrey Eaton."

That was the last night I was ever to sleep with my husband.

It seems impossible that until now I have not stopped to give thanks for this gift, this lifetime of solace.

seven

August 20

I left the hotel too late and then made the mother of wrong turns. I ended up driving in what seemed like circles and never managed to find the church. I was downright mad when I finally decided to give it up. I would have missed half the service anyway, not to mention the fact that my spirit was woefully unfit for worship. This is the first time I've loused up so badly. I drove back to the hotel after stopping for directions—at two convenience stores I might add—and put my car away. Walking seemed prudent today.

After chilling awhile in front of the television, I took the riverboat tour, a San Antonio equivalent of my Dallas trolley ride, and that, plus the peacefulness of my room, helped restore me to my senses. I found a seat in the boat and told God, hoping he'd see the humor in it, that I would worship this Sunday in a boat like so many do. When the tour was completed and I arrived back where I started, I headed to the glass mall, imposingly huge as well as intriguing. I doubt I would have gone if I hadn't been desperate for makeup. Because I'm getting so good at reading any sort of map, aside from today's significant lapse, I found a department store and the counter I needed in a relatively short amount of time. It restored my confidence to a degree.

The clerk, this one quite pleasant, rifled through the drawers and quickly handed me the liquid foundation and mascara I asked for, but because the powers that be keep retiring any shade of lipstick I prefer, we spent a lot of time together looking for something I could tolerate. I use a significant amount of makeup, but the effect is nothing if not subtle. I choose earth tones for my eyes, eschewing bright eye shadows; smoky is as adventurous as my eyes get. I wear color on my cheeks, enough to look healthy, but I have an unreasonable and unyielding aversion to lip color. This clerk seemed to understand that no amount of cajoling or flattery could convince me to wear anything on my lips in the red or brown family, or even pink and most peaches. The fact that Plush Nude was the name of my discontinued lipstick made an impression on her.

"You don't want a sticky gloss," she said, putting the cylinder she had just shown me away. "What you're looking for is a moist lipstick with a little shine but only the slightest touch of color."

"Exactly!" I said.

I wanted to give her a gold star.

Each of us leaned over our respective side of the counter, drawing lines of potential candidates across the back of my hand. A counter covered with no less than twenty different testers and a colorful wad of Kleenex testified to our tenacity. We were Audrey and Ginger long before I handed her my credit card.

"You should have my name," Ginger said, nodding at my hair. "Is that natural?"

"So far," I said.

"I change my color at least once a month," she said, "but if I had your auburn hair and those eyes not far from the same color, I'd never fool with it."

"Well, thanks," I said.

We turned our attention to yet another tester, and I felt like I had a friend by the time I found something I could live with. The lipstick I finally chose is called Shhh. That struck me as so appropriate for the life I've been leading that I bought three. Ginger seemed pleased.

It was almost dark when I left the mall. As I walked over to ride the elevator to the top of the Tower of the Americas and view the lights of the city from 750 feet, I thought how nice it was to have Ginger helping me this afternoon. A gentle breeze made the heat tolerable when I stepped out on the observation deck, and I found places for an unobstructed view of all the points of interest. If it wasn't a feast for my eyes, it was a nice Sunday meal, and a good way to end a day that started so badly.

Or it would have been.

When I came back to my room and tossed my keys into my purse, I noticed my sack of makeup wasn't in the large outside pocket where I had placed it for safekeeping.

What could I have done with it?

When I left Ginger, I went straight to the tower and then to the hotel, except for a quick stop in the parking lot to get my shoe bag from the car.

I dumped the contents of my purse on the bed, thinking I might have put the sack inside the purse and not remembered doing it. I found a pair of earrings, a laminated bookmark Kelsie had made me in kindergarten, a ticket stub from *South Pacific*, and salt packets, but not a sack of cosmetics. I checked the shoe bag in case I had put it in there for some crazy reason. Nothing. I was so disgusted. I had spent a ridiculous amount of time selecting that makeup, and besides that, I needed it.

I decided to check the car. Maybe it had fallen on the floor when I grabbed the shoe bag. I even checked the trunk, though I hadn't opened the thing. By the time I finished ransacking the car, I was agitated beyond reason. I retraced my steps to the tower, willing the little package to be waiting for me on the floor in a dark spot along the railing somewhere. I walked around the circumference of the deserted tower twice, but if I had dropped my sack of makeup there, someone had already returned the lipstick for something with more color. I stood there trying to calm down, telling myself there was no reason whatsoever to be so disgusted, frantic even, about losing some makeup.

Can someone explain why I leaned against the wall, looked out at the lights of San Antonio, and sobbed as though I had lost something very dear?

I walked into the hotel hiding my swollen, bloodshot eyes behind sunglasses. I rushed to my room, washed my face, and lay down with a cold washcloth on my eyes, trying underneath the soothing terry cloth to fathom what the last hour had been about. I had been a runaway train, crashing at the top of the Tower of the Americas. There was no making sense of it.

I finally stood up, hung the washcloth in the bathroom, put on my gown, and picked up Tom's Bible on my way back to the bed. I flipped to a highlighted passage in John 4 and had the patience to read all of one verse: "My food," Jesus says, "is to do the will of him who sent me and to finish his work."

What is *my* food? What nourishes and satisfies me? What can I not live without? The madness of the last hour suggests the answer is makeup.

Doing God's will is the last thing I've been concerned about lately.

Or is it?

Perhaps his will for me right now is to learn how to live without Tom, to learn to live with what is left, to somehow quit mourning "the tender grace of a day that is dead" and instead embrace and celebrate "the tender grace of a day," each one a gift from an eminently good God.

Could I get that intravenously?

August 21

I like to ease into the morning. Dawdling suits me.

Not Tom. He liked to get up while the birds were still warming up for their early morning concert. He would have his shower taken, the paper read, and his cereal eaten before the *Today* show began. He saw a good many sunrises in his lifetime. I've seen few and have wished embracing the morning was as natural for me as it was for Tom.

He was always the first one to school. He was usually in his office thirty minutes before anyone else arrived, setting a fine example for the faculty and staff. His favorite saying, pulled out when he was encouraging punctuality, was "If you aren't ten minutes early, you're late." By this standard I was always late when I rushed into my first class with ten *seconds* to spare.

This was an issue we never resolved. Our last argument had to do with this discrepancy in our personalities and took place on a Sunday only a month or so before he died.

"It's seven thirty," he said as I sat at my vanity running a comb through my wet hair.

Grrr. This was a warning, not information. A clock sat on my vanity, less than two feet from my face.

"Don't do that, Tom," I said. "I'll either be ready when you leave the house at eight fifteen or I won't. We can take both cars if we need to."

At 8:16 I was ready and glad to see he was still in the house, standing by the door leading to the garage. He even smiled.

Why I always insisted on cutting it so close, I cannot say. I don't like that about myself. He probably didn't either.

I intended to leave for Austin today, but I didn't leave this room. After what happened this morning, I decided to dawdle away the entire day.

I got up late and headed for the shower, still thinking I would leave today.

But standing under the cascading water, I began to cry. I would have thought after last night my reservoir of tears would be depleted. Crying eventually turned into sobbing, gasping-for-breath sobbing. I stopped only long enough to shout something I haven't uttered since I left home: "I don't want this. I *do not* want this!"

When I could finally stop crying, I turned off the water, wrapped a towel around me, walked to the unmade bed as though I were sleepwalking, fell onto it, and stared with unseeing eyes at the ceiling.

Then, with nothing on but a towel, I tugged at the comforter and pulled it over me and fell into a deep sleep. I awoke an hour later, disoriented until the towel and my damp hair reminded me of my meltdown. Management had not knocked on my door, so I assume running water and well-insulated walls muffled the outburst.

After the craziness of last night, I had pulled myself together enough to write an entry that ended with a sliver of optimism. But this morning I wanted, more than anything I can think of, for Tom to walk into the bathroom and say that we were going to be late if I didn't hurry up. I've finally figured out that the obvious antecedent for the ambiguous pronoun in "I don't want this" is the infinitive phrase "to live life without Tom."

I do not want to live life without Tom!

I just don't.

That I have no choice doesn't seem to give me the perspective it should.

⌒

I've been thinking that maybe letting go of what we had is so hard because the last decade of our marriage was so good. Each decade seemed to get better.

Not that the first ten years weren't okay, but most couples have issues to deal with those first years, don't they? I used to beat myself up for any tension we experienced early on until I finally accepted that blending two personalities, two backgrounds, two histories, two agendas probably isn't easy for most people.

A benign example is the budget. Both of us agreed that our bills should be paid and something should be put in a savings account. The argument was how much should be put in savings and how much should remain at our disposal. The first year we were married we had a dandy tiff about whether we could get an unplanned pizza one school night. Those issues get resolved eventually, and two do "become one" in ways other than physical. I can't remember the last time the budget or any financial matter was an issue.

What I consider our worst argument also occurred and recurred in the first decade. I made a hateful accusation, trying, I'm sure, to defend myself unnecessarily. I had failed to do something I said I'd do, or maybe it was the time I lost a hundred dollar bill, our grocery money for a week. Whatever it was, Tom said I should have been more careful, or something of that nature. I do, however, recall my exact words.

"So sorry, Tom," I snapped, slamming a book down on the kitchen table. "I wish I could be *perfect* like you!"

It was a meanness spoken out of my frustration with my own lack of perfection, or anything close to it. I apologized, of course. He never said he was perfect, and I never had reason to believe he thought it either. Instead he was energetic and conscientious, qualities I admired and envied, and qualities that blessed my life. The bills were always paid, the grass always mowed, golf dates with friends and promises to grandchildren always kept. I never ceased to be amazed that he could do everything he was supposed to do when he was supposed to do it and with so little effort.

Doing what I'm supposed to do when I'm supposed to do it has always taxed me. That has threatened my contentment from time to time. When I once vented something of this nature to Molly, she was incensed. She said I always graded my mound of papers on time and with great care, that I made our home a beautiful and comfortable sanctuary, and that my humor, sensitivity and kindness (the insecure memorize indirect compliments) made my children and their father whole and happy. But I know what I know: Tom made life both good and easy for me.

Sometimes I wonder which is greater, grief or fear.

eight

August 22

I did not dawdle this morning. I took a shower without incident, rushed to the mall to replace my makeup (Ginger was surprised to see me and cheered when she found one last tube of Shhh), and drove to Austin. As soon as I was settled in the Holiday Inn Express, I Googled *Austin* and confirmed what I had suspected: The city was not named for any of my father's ancestors. Nevertheless, it looked like a nice city. I took a walking tour of important sites this morning and then grabbed a pretzel and a Diet Coke and spent more time on a self-guided tour, enjoying the serendipity of exploring old neighborhoods, especially the historic district with its beautiful Victorian homes.

Returning to the car, I happened to pass a school where classrooms of elementary children were emptying systematically into the playground and front lawn. I heard an alarm but saw no flames or smoke and assumed I was watching a fire drill. Strangely enough, that capped off my day. It took me back to the first time I'd laid eyes on Tom Eaton.

I had just graduated and accepted my first teaching job. Tom, assistant principal at the time, had been away working on his doctorate when I was interviewed and subsequently hired that spring, and he was gone again the opening days of school. I had not met or seen him, but he apparently had heard about me, had seen me, and even knew where my room was located.

Rumors were rampant one day in late September that there would be either a fire or a tornado drill that afternoon, and I very much wanted to impress my students and the administration with my maturity and responsibility. The three short blasts of the alarm sounded for all the world like the description of the tornado drill, so I told my students to file out of the door and into the hall and to sit in front of the lockers with their heads between their knees. They did this in record time, and I couldn't have been more proud.

Pride left in a huff, however, when I finally noticed other students marching toward the exit at the end of the long hall and at the same time noticed the expression on the face of an extremely handsome man who had materialized, dressed professionally in khaki pants, a white long-sleeved dress shirt, and red paisley tie.

He pointed to the exit and said, "This is a fire drill, Miss Austin."

I was mortified.

"Okay, then," I said. "Let's go, kids."

The next morning as I was screeching into my room just before the bell rang, he met me outside my door, explained he was the assistant principal, and asked me to drop by his office during my planning period.

He was packing his things into a cardboard box when I found his office.

I tapped on his open door. "I haven't driven you away, have I?"

I heard his laugh for the first time.

I thought he had called me in to tell me I had ruined the school record for time required for students to exit the building during a fire drill. Instead he began to explain that he was being transferred to another high school to replace a principal who had suffered a serious stroke.

I was disappointed he wouldn't be outside my classroom door again. The thought of him had been making me smile, which seemed a miracle to me.

I couldn't have been more shocked when he said he was glad for the unexpected change in his plans. "That will allow me to call you sometime, if you don't mind."

A week later he did. That Christmas he asked me to marry him, and in July he became my husband.

Today I looked at more highlighted verses in John 4. Jesus heals an official's son simply by speaking the words, "Your son will live."

How I wish he would have said such a thing to me. "Your husband will live."

I've always believed Jesus did such things so that people would realize he was sent from God, who is near and able, but I imagine many reading this account are like the official: It is not the joy of knowing God and belonging to him they want, but his miracle. Except for a very few, the fleeting physical is far more significant than the spiritual, even though it is eternal.

I have to admit that transcending the physical is not easy for me either. Look no further than yesterday morning and my version of a *Psycho* shower scene.

August 23

A dream awoke me in the early morning. The digital clock said 3:45. It's not the first time I've dreamed of Tom. In one dream I walked out of the high school building just in time to see a school bus pulling away from the curb. Tom, who to my knowledge never drove a school bus, was sitting in the driver's seat. He had told me nothing about a trip. I tried to catch the bus to ask where he was going and when he'd be back, but he didn't see me. I stood in the middle of the street watching until it was a yellow dot in the distance.

In another dream he was walking on a long, narrow beam high in the rafters of a barn, his arms extended for balance.

I stood below, begging him to come down, but he laughed and said he was fine, that I shouldn't worry.

In last night's dream, he was where he was supposed to be, asleep in his recliner. When I came into the living room, I walked over to him and put my hand on his face. When he opened his eyes and smiled, relief flooded me. I told him to get up and come to bed. He put the remote on the round table beside his chair and said okay, but when I got to the bedroom door and turned around, he wasn't there.

That's when I woke up. I lay there a long time staring into the darkness before I got up and walked into the bathroom to find something to help me sleep. I stood in the glare of the bathroom light looking at the little blue pill in the palm of my hand and decided I would try to sleep without it. I would give myself a half hour.

As I waited for the thirty minutes to transpire, I grabbed the Bible I had put on the bedside table and turned to some verses in the fifth chapter, where Jesus comes across a man who has been an invalid for thirty-eight years. What struck me as I read this at four in the morning was what Jesus asked the man before he healed him: "Do you want to get well?"

What a strange question.

I really do wonder why he asked him that. Surely the man wanted to get well. But after I turned out the light and closed my eyes, the same question came to me: *Audrey, do you want to get well?*

I thought the question was rhetorical, but lying there staring into the dark, I realized it really wasn't, and I lay there for several minutes before I had my answer. Rolling over and pulling the sheet over my shoulder, I finally whispered, "Yes, I do."

I think I at last understood why I love my Indian sculpture so much. I'm drawn to his posture. It suggests a wisdom that knows where his help comes from and a humility to ask for it. He stands there gratefully anticipating blessings from the Source of all good things. If an artist thought to create a contrast to that pose, I would be a good model, at least in the months since Tom died. I've offered only generic petitions from the fetal position.

~

I spent the afternoon at an art museum housed in a renovated villa on Lake Austin. I had worn a white one-piece cotton knit dress that hit me, as usual, at midcalf (an excellent length for my legs). A wide brown belt slung around my hips, an attempt at accessorizing, gave it a casual but stylish look. It's one of several things I've brought with me that says—with a hint of a smile—I'm much too young to be a grandmother. Yet it was close enough to age appropriate, especially considering the girl who stopped me as I wandered about the grounds.

She had on a jean skirt that covered maybe an inch of her long, thin legs; two complementary tank tops under a cropped jacket; and wedge sandals that made her at least five foot eleven. The censuring mother and teacher in me grudgingly admitted she looked adorable. For the first time I felt like AARP should actually be sending me their unsolicited materials.

"Do you have the time?" she asked.

I looked at my watch and told her it was just after four thirty. Suddenly she grabbed my wrist and stared at my hand.

"That is *exactly* what I've been looking for," she said.

She glanced around, spotted her boyfriend across the way, and called to him.

"Brent," she said as he walked up. "Look at this woman's ring. This is what I want."

I surmised I was looking at a couple about to become engaged.

"I'm afraid you can't have it," I told her with a smile.

She laughed. "I mean one *like* it. What's it called?"

"It's a marquise."

"It's perfect."

"My husband has wonderful taste," I told her. "In all these years, I've never seen anything I like more."

Her boyfriend dutifully noted the size and cut of my diamond and then started leading his future wife toward an older couple standing nearby and the parking lot beyond them.

"Thanks so much," she said over her shoulder.

"You're quite welcome," I said as they hurried away. I'm sure if she had anything to say about it, they would be in a jewelry store within the hour.

I got in the car a few minutes later and drove to a place

where I could park by the lake. I got out of the car, leaned against it, and drank in the calm beauty of the water. Then I held out my hand and looked at my ring, more beautiful than it was the night I opened the little gray box and looked down at it for the first time.

"I did it again," I whispered.

I had spoken of Tom in the present tense.

Do you want to get well?

There is probably a sense in which I will always think of Tom in the present tense, but he is not sitting at home in his recliner or working in his garden or waiting for me back at the hotel.

Except to have it cleaned or a prong repaired, I hadn't taken off my ring since Tom slipped it on my finger over thirty-two years ago. Closing my eyes as if in prayer, I stood in the warmth of the sun and worked it off my finger.

Gift of love and promise, the ring didn't travel far—I merely moved it to the ring finger of my right hand. There it will remain until the day I die.

August 24

I could hardly do the Lyndon B. Johnson State Park and Historic Site justice in one day, but I did what I could. It seemed the least I could do, penance for wondering in my youth if LBJ had something to do with the assassination of President Kennedy.

At the farmstead I spent some time with a guy dressed in period clothing pounding horseshoes on an anvil. He might have been thirty or sixty—I couldn't tell behind the beard—but he was more talkative than I imagined a blacksmith "back then" would have been. On the other hand, it was I, the only visitor in the vicinity at the time, who unaccountably started the exchange.

"So," I said when I walked over to where he worked at one end of the barn, "you must be the resident blacksmith."

"Sure am," he said. "You like horses?"

"Sure," I said, keeping it simple. "Looking at them anyway."

He began to tell me all kinds of horse facts, including how often the animals need to have their hooves trimmed—I think he said every six weeks!

"My goodness," I told him as I headed toward the open doors of the barn to find the farmhouse, "their feet need more maintenance than mine."

"Yep," he said, pounding away.

It seems to me the jobs on a farm at the turn of the century were difficult and endless, and while I might find that life fascinating, I can't imagine that I could have possibly been fit for it. If I'd been Laura's mother, stuck in a little house on the prairie, I'm afraid the kids and I would have died the first winter while Pa took too much time in town getting our meager supplies and having his horse shod. If Molly were here, she'd probably pop up with some objection, but I'm more realistic about my limitations than she.

Sometimes driving by the take-out window of Taco Bell seems taxing.

⤳

The right word for how I feel just now eludes me.

After I did my reading, I went online to write the kids and was surprised to find two messages in my in-box that weren't from Mark or Molly.

One was from Willa. She said she had been calling and calling, and what was up with that? Finally she called Molly and learned that I was on a trip, somewhere in the middle of Texas at the moment. I don't see how I could have overlooked her name when I sent out the group e-mail saying I'd be gone and unavailable for a while.

"CALL ME!!!" she wrote. "At least answer this e-mail. I want to know what's going on! Plus, I need to tell you something!"

Willa's favorite end punctuation is the exclamation mark. In high school she passed a one-page note in first-hour biology, and I counted no fewer than twenty-five of them. Exclaiming is a strand in her DNA.

I really thought I might be home before Willa had time to worry about my trip. We've gone as long as two months without talking to each other, though I guess it hasn't happened often in the forty years since I first met Willa Kay Ball in PE on the first day of high school.

We bonded almost instantly, because, despite her surname, we shared an abhorrence for any activity with the word *ball* attached to it: basketball, softball, volleyball, even dodgeball. We hated even more the gym clothes issued to us by our irrationally proper PE teacher, and we hated the locker room scene more than that. It was my misfortune to know no one when I walked into the gym that morning. Or maybe it wasn't, because when I plopped on the first row of bleachers beside Miss Ball, she recognized something in Miss Austin and soon became my best friend.

That our fathers were both named William might have furthered our bond. Her mother, having heard of the author Willa Cather, thought Willa the perfect name for her only child.

"Why, oh why," Willa lamented many times during our high school years, "couldn't my mother have named me Audrey? Or Pam?"

I never had an answer for her, really, but I did say once that there are worse names. For a girl with the last name of Ball, Lucille came to mind.

Willa's message I didn't mind so much; in fact, I was almost glad to hear from her, exclamations and all. It was the other message that upset me. I didn't recognize the address and there was no subject line, so I almost deleted it and wished I had when I saw who wrote it.

I haven't spoken to Andrew Ackerman in twenty-seven years. His message was proper and brief, but even so, I considered it an intrusion.

"I ran into Willa," he wrote, "and she told me about your husband. I'm sorry. Andrew."

nine

August 25

I slept late and wanted to sleep later still. Once I bothered to open my eyes, I lounged in bed with the remote until I couldn't find one program capable of keeping, of even capturing, my interest. When I threw the covers back shortly before noon, I actually considered packing the car and driving home.

But that had as many cons as pros. And there's this: It didn't seem the right thing to do.

Before I hit the shower, I did something as unlikely as hurrying to the mall to buy a hip-hop CD: I put on my bathing suit and cover-up and went to the pool. Expecting solitude at that time of day, I stretched out on a white plastic lounger and, with an SPF 25 sunblock and sunglasses to protect my face, lay back to soak up the sun for a little while.

I hadn't been settled more than a minute when a high-pitched question shattered my hope of solitude.

"Do you mind if I splash you?"

She must have been underwater when I arrived, or quietly contemplating life treading water near the edge of the pool, but now she peeked over the edge of the pool, looking right at me, asking a ridiculous question. She appeared to be four or five, just a bit younger than Jada and Kelsie, and she had crayon-red hair and a face full of freckles.

I told her I didn't much want to be splashed, but I smiled when I said it. I was considering leaving a place that had only promised peace when she dog-paddled to the steps, marched dramatically up each one of them, and stretched out on the lounger next to mine, her hands clasped behind her head.

"What brings you to Austin?" she asked.

I wondered if she was doing a round-up article for *USA Today*. Then I decided I'd give her as good an answer as I had.

"The Lord," I said.

"I'm here for a family reunion. Everybody wants to see me because there are fourteen grandchildren and I'm the only girl!"

"Wow," I said.

I asked her where her mother was, though it seemed possible this child had taken a cab from wherever she came from and checked herself into the presidential suite.

"Mom had to go to the bathroom," the little girl explained.

"We don't pee in the pool," she added, scrunching her nose and shaking her head at the thought.

Before I could think of a response, I heard the iron gate clang and saw a woman with red hair and a sprinkling of freckles rushing toward us.

"Helen," she yelled, "I thought you were right behind me!"

I doubt four children could be more trouble than Helen.

"Mom," Helen said, "the Lord brought this lady to our hotel."

The woman said, "What?"

I almost laughed at my quandary. Ah, what to say to Helen's mother.

"Your daughter told me," I began, "that you're here for a family reunion."

She nodded.

"Well, I'm just here. Which is strange for me. I usually have a flesh-and-blood companion and an agenda."

I felt like I was elaborating more than necessary or desirable. Nevertheless, I continued like I didn't have good sense.

"And since I don't think I'm ever really alone, despite how it looks, I told Helen the Lord brought me."

"See, Mom!"

Abruptly Helen jumped up and hollered, "Watch this!"

She ran to the edge of the pool and cannonballed into

the middle of it, soaking her mother and me and a fifty-foot radius of concrete.

"Helen Eugenia!" her mother scolded. "What are you thinking?"

Helen smiled from the middle of the pool. "Sorry," she said, not looking in the least bit sorry.

Her mother turned to me and apologized for Helen's exuberance.

"I can't say the water didn't feel good," I said, magnanimous since I hadn't done my hair yet. "Besides, exuberance is too rare and thrilling to censure completely, isn't it?"

Her mom smiled at Helen and then at me, the woman the Lord had brought to Austin.

Oh well, either Helen's mother understood what I had said or she didn't. Besides, she had her hands full with Helen. While I collected my towel and sunblock, heading to my room to clean up, Helen yelled "Bye" and in the same breath begged her mother to come in the water and play whales with her.

I walked away thinking how much Tom would have enjoyed talking to Helen. Though he was a high school principal, talking with young children was one of his greatest delights.

I had walked out to the garden unnoticed one May afternoon and watched him showing a then three-year-old Kelsie how to plant tomatoes.

"I'll pour the water, Papa," she said when he had scooped out the soil and set a new plant into the hole he had dug.

He handed her a plastic cup and held the plant straight

while she poured the mixture of water and Miracle-Gro around it. When he began to push the soil back around the plant, she knelt beside him and said, "I'll help you, Papa." And she, as gently as her grandpa had done, patted the soil around the plant until it was secure.

"Good job," he said, kissing the top of her head. Kelsie stood up and stretched like Tom did and saw me standing at the gate with her baby brother on my hip. "We're making tomatoes," she said, beaming.

On this August afternoon, I slipped my key into the slot and admitted to myself that Helen had been a pleasant intrusion.

August 26

I've wondered how much easier this trip might have been if my car had one of those navigation systems. At the same time, I rather like my atlas. I opened it to Texas and laid it out before me on the bed last night to look at my options. I decided I could make it all the way to Amarillo today, a seven- or eight-hour drive according to my rudimentary calculations.

Make that twelve hours, when you count the four hours I sat on the side of the road.

Between Austin and Amarillo there might be five miles that don't have cell phone coverage, and that is where the blowout occurred. I was able to get the car to the side of the road, for which I gave thanks, but when my cell phone didn't work, I began to panic. I am sorry to admit that, at fifty-five years of age, I have never changed a tire or had a lesson on how to change one. Tom tried to show me once, but I didn't want to fool with it. I always assumed Step One, join AAA, Step Two, get a cell phone, and Step Three, pay your bill.

The road was not busy today, but the cars that were on the road zipped by like my Solara and I didn't exist. It was discouraging at first, and then maddening. I'm happy to say my irritation did not escalate to using inappropriate language or hand motions. I told myself, *Surely some kind soul will call the highway patrol when he or she gets close enough to a tower for a cell phone to work.*

But nooooo.

Two hours later, I was thinking about opening the trunk and seeing if I could find a jack and intuit how to get it on my car. What kind of death did I want to die?

My answer was pulling over in his beat-up pickup truck.

"Got a problem?" he asked, spitting tobacco on the side of the road and wiping sweat off his forehead with the back of his hand.

I hoped that question wouldn't prove to be ironic.

"It's a hot one," he added

I looked at his black hat, black shirt, black jeans, and black boots and thought a man driving without an air-conditioner might consider wearing white. He didn't smile, and his truck and demeanor didn't comfort me.

He bent over and looked at my right back tire. Finally he smiled. "This ain't good."

"Do you happen to have a cell phone?" I asked.

He laughed.

"Mine doesn't work out here, I'm afraid."

"Well," he said, rolling up his sleeves, "let's get you taken care of."

"Oh, thank you!" I gushed, but he was in the trunk pulling out the jack and spare and didn't appear to hear me.

"So," I said while he made short work of replacing the old tire with the spare, "do you live around here?"

"Over in Nazareth," he said.

"Nazareth? Well, my goodness."

We didn't talk much after that, but when he had the tire on, the jack removed, and everything where it was supposed to be in the trunk, every bit as neatly as I would have done it, he said, "Well, you're fixed up."

I wanted to hug him, but that seemed rather inappropriate.

"I'd like to pay you," I said, reaching through the driver's window for my purse.

"I won't take nothing," he said, heading back to his truck.

"But, sir," I said. He turned and looked at me, and I wondered why I had stopped him. He wouldn't take recompense, and I had no words to thank him for coming to my rescue, for saving me more trouble than I could imagine. But I had to say *something*.

"I hope someone helps someone you love someday."

"They already have, ma'am. You be careful now."

"I will. You too."

I stood waiting for him to leave until I realized he wasn't budging until I was on the road. He followed me a few miles to the next intersection, and I waved when he turned off, and I asked God to go with him to Nazareth. The cowboy in black actually made me glad I had a tire to replace, time to make up, and an unwarranted scare.

It was late when I hauled my stuff inside the hotel and ate peanut butter and cheese sandwich crackers I'd purchased from a machine down the hall. I was starving. Relishing the crackers, I thought it was appropriate that I flipped to John 6, where Jesus is feeding over five thousand hungry mouths with no vending machine, just a little boy's five small loaves of bread and two fish.

After everyone was fed, Jesus tells the disciples to "gather the pieces that are left over. Let nothing be wasted."

In God's economy, it appears nothing is wasted. Could that include the nothingness of my last fifteen months? Could that mean a flat tire, or even a warning ticket? Could it mean a frightening clerk or a friendly one? An Indian sculpture or a grieving mother? A cowboy from Nazareth?

When I opened my laptop to tell Molly and Mark about tonight's reading, there was a message from Willa. I had answered her last night in as few words as possible, a study in short, simple sentences: "I'm fine. I just needed to get 'out.'

I decide where I'm going from day to day. I'll be in Amarillo tomorrow. I'll keep you posted."

I should have realized she'd have a message waiting for me.

"If you don't stop in Phoenix, I will hate you forever!!!"

After that introductory statement, she went on to tell me they had just opened the house. She and Ed, who is semi-retired now and consulting when something good comes along, still spend their summers in Iowa, but they built a house in Phoenix two years ago and spend the other nine months there. She had seen Andrew when they were out to dinner last weekend. She had forgotten he lived there, if she ever knew it.

"Until he literally backed into me in the crowded vestibule," she wrote, "I hadn't seen him since our twentieth reunion, the one you refused to attend."

Willa always has her own take on things.

"Anyway," she said, "when Drew asked about you, I told him about Tom. I hope that's okay."

"No problem," I wrote back. "And I'll see about Phoenix."

I could have said, *I wish you had told him nothing about me. If he ever asks again, tell him I don't exist.*

He doesn't either. Tell him that too.

ten

August 27

I designated today as Weird Day, and not counting what I'd call a wonderful church service in a beautiful and expansive new structure not far from my hotel, it was.

For years I've seen a billboard on a stretch of I-44 near home advertising a free seventy-two-ounce steak. The first time I saw it, I turned to Tom in amazement and exclaimed like Willa, "It's in *Amarillo*, Tom!" I just couldn't fathom an advertisement for something that far away. The size of the steak, of course, struck me as amazing too. Make that horrifying. I usually have to work at eating an eight-ounce fillet.

Today I made it to the Big Texan Steak Ranch and felt like I had done something. I walked through the doors and thought, *Here I am, Tom*.

It was long before the dinner crowd would descend, so

the man behind the bar, dressed much like the cowboy who had rescued me on the side of the road, looked up and gave me an Amarillo welcome.

"So," I said, flopping my purse on the bar between us, "can I get a hamburger basket to go?"

He handed me the Big Texan menu, shaped like a giant trifolded one hundred dollar bill. "Oh, honey, we can do better than that!"

I looked at the brown and white menu he handed me and had to smile at the *Rick Was Here* scrawled across the front of it in green crayon. Well, Rick, so was Audrey.

"Look here," Bar Guy said, opening the menu and pointing at a row of appetizers, "why get a plain ol' hamburger when you can have fried rattlesnake or buffalo quesadillas."

"Oh, I don't think so," I said. "I'm rather craving a hamburger."

He was much too pleasant to press it, and soon he called over a cute little waitress to take my boring order back to the kitchen. That's when I learned Bar Guy's name was Wayne, as in "Sure 'nuff, Wayne." While I waited, Wayne took me into the huge dining room and showed me the table, center stage, where thousands of people have tried to eat the seventy-two-ounce steak with all the trimmings in an hour, the requirement for getting it free. I don't recall the sign I'd seen back home mentioning that technicality.

"You sure you don't want to try it," he asked, "instead of taking home a measly hamburger basket?"

"I'm sure. *So* sure."

"Well, at least let me take your picture sitting behind the table with that timer over your head. It'll make a good one."

I told him I didn't have my camera with me. He thought that was a shame, but a party of eight or so was coming through the door, and he had to get back to his post. I was able to escape with my burger basket a few minutes later, waving at Wayne on my way out. The home of the free seventy-two-ounce steak is quite a colorful place, and I'm not sorry I went there.

I can't say that about the Cadillac Ranch on down the interstate. According to Wayne, it was something I should see, and I did, but from behind my windshield. Getting out of the car didn't seem necessary. For once, I'm not sad that Tom missed something I've now seen.

⌒

My level of activity has increased dramatically since I left home, but I still seem to tire easily and I want to curl up on the bed and watch television. That is what I planned for tonight, what I still plan for tonight, but first I read a passage from Tom's Bible and checked my e-mail.

Checking e-mail isn't as simple as it used to be. Now when I click on the envelope icon, I don't assume I'll hear from only Mark and Molly. I expect Willa to continue badgering me until I write in my blood that I've put Phoenix on my list of destinations. And although his note gave no indication that he would, I've been afraid Andrew would write again.

Today he did.

"I didn't hear from you," he said. "I hope you're okay."

Two lines came to me from the old Phil Collins song "Separate Lives": "You have no right to ask me how I feel; you have no right to speak to me so kind."

I thought about writing those lines as a reply. But I chose no reply at all. Doesn't silence mean *go away*?

Probably not to Andrew. His picture is by the word *charm* in Webster's. No one ever sent him away. I doubt that has changed.

He used to tell our eleventh-grade language arts teacher every single day that she had on a "lovely ensemble." And every single day she laughed. It was their little joke, though the rest of us laughed along with them. He was the president of our junior class, and it seemed like every student and teacher knew Drew Ackerman and liked him. Language arts was the first class I had with him, though I was hardly aware of it since Mrs. Henry, hard as this is to imagine, seated us in alphabetical order. He sat in the first seat of the first row. I landed three seats behind him, after Sarah Allen and Billy Atwood. Willa, my main entertainment in that class, sat behind me.

It was in Mrs. Henry's class that he first noticed me. We were starting a poetry unit, and Mrs. Henry asked if we could name an emotion a poem had aroused in us.

I thought of one in two seconds and took the opportunity to raise my hand.

"Miss Austin?"

"Fear," I said.

"Fear?"

She must have been expecting something else.

"When I was in the eighth grade," I explained, "my English teacher, Mr. Belk, closed the blinds, turned out the lights, and walked up and down the aisles quoting 'The Raven.' In the blackness, he bent down and stage-whispered a *nevermore* right behind me, and I almost fell out of my desk."

"So, you're saying Poe's 'Raven' had the power to elicit fear from you?"

"Yes, I think it did. But not as much as Mr. Belk did."

"No kidding!" Willa said, evidently caught up in the image.

Mrs. Henry smiled at both of us and moved on to the next raised hand. Meanwhile, Drew Ackerman leaned out of his seat, looked back at me, and smiled. He looked at me so long and so intently that Willa nudged me when he turned back around.

That was our only meaningful encounter until our senior year.

It was a lifetime ago.

I do not want to go there.

Instead I'll think about the passage I read earlier.

The disciples are in rough waters three or four miles from shore on the Sea of Galilee when they see someone walking toward them on the water. They are terrified until Jesus says, "It is I; don't be afraid."

The comforting words of Jesus resonated with me.

Two other verses came to me, also perfect for calming the rough waters of my soul, and I added them to my promise verse of the last fifteen months. Together, I think they have the capacity to dispense the calm and courage I need so much: "I will fear no evil, for you are with me"; "It is I; don't be afraid"; "I am with you always"; "I will never leave you nor forsake you."

When I find it hard to sleep, these verses will be the sheep I count.

August 28

"When do you think you'll be here?" Willa asked.

I read that and gasped.

"You know the casita is like your own little apartment," she continued. "You know I've always supported whatever you need to do. You know I'll give you your space."

The last time I stayed in their casita, Tom was with me. The four of us played golf in the mornings, though Willa and I merely rode in the golf carts and putted, played cards in the evening after dinner, and relaxed in their hot tub under the stars late at night before Tom and I took ourselves out to the casita and made love like we were at an upscale resort on an exotic island. Can I enter that suite without him?

Willa was right, though, she does give me space, and given an exuberance that almost matches little Helen's, that's saying something. And she has always supported my decisions, most notably the one to transfer to SMSU in Springfield after our sophomore year at Oklahoma State University. This support was no small thing for Willa; we were two of four girls sharing an apartment together and loving it. The fact that she had met Ed Foster and was spending any free time with him might have made my decision easier for her; nevertheless, I appreciated her making that break less painful for me.

She put Ed on hold while we worked in our room, gathering my things, packing them in suitcases and boxes.

She attempted conversation. "I can't believe you're leaving me here alone. Summer school will be horrible without you!"

"Ed is still here. It won't be horrible."

"Your aunt won't be as much fun as I am," she said.

"That goes without saying, but she's very nice. You know that."

Actually, we talked little during the hours we packed up two years of my college life. We both knew this move was drastic, but I would not put myself in the position of running into Andrew again.

I stared at Willa's message for a while; then I wrote her that I would come for a few days, but I could not tell her when. That would have to be good enough.

⌒

I have planned for years to take violin lessons when I get to heaven. I told Tom he'd find me practicing in the far northwest corner if he needed me. But since I'm pretty sure I'll be a slow learner, I said he might not want to trek back there for the first ten thousand years or so.

My children, like their father, could hardly fathom my devotion to orchestras, and parts thereof. Even a cello solo used to thrill me. Tom loved music, but he only attended concerts featuring something like a string quartet for me. I reveled in those hours; he simply tried to stay awake. This evening, thanks to the Amarillo Opera, I had the chance to combine two former interests: botanical gardens and stringed instruments. I brought a blanket from the hotel and left it in the car until I retrieved it for Music in the Gardens, which took place in the amphitheater at seven thirty. I actually felt something resembling excitement at the thought of hearing the classical violin and cello.

I finished strolling through the garden in time to find a strategic spot for my blanket. Hardly anyone was there when I arrived, but it wasn't long before blankets and lawn chairs were filling up the space around me. I looked at a young couple down from me, talking and drinking their gourmet coffee, and decided if they turned around and noticed me sitting alone, I could say, *My husband will be back in just a minute.*

What a nut I am.

Not long before the concert began, an elderly gentleman, easing his way through the maze of blankets and chairs with his wife, tripped and fell to his knees practically onto my blanket. I hated that for him. And it scared me.

"Sir," I said, reaching out to him, "are you okay?"

He made a production of feeling the bones in his arms and legs and said, "Well, young lady"—it must have been the outfit—"everything but my pride seems remarkably intact, despite this little mishap."

I stood up and, together with his wife, helped him to his feet.

"Would you like to share my blanket?" I asked. I really thought they should get settled. They both thanked me profusely but said they were looking for their children, who should have chairs for them. Apparently they were supposed to be in this area.

"Do you want me to help you look for them?"

I hardly got the question out of my mouth before I heard a deep voice calling, "Dad! Mom!" A man about my age, maybe somewhat older, weaved his way toward us and put his arms around each of his parents. I was happy they'd been found.

"Enjoy the concert, sir," I said as they turned with their son to find the rest of the family and two sturdy chairs to sit in. The old man, his thick white hair shining, his eyes lively and kind, came back and took my hand.

"Call me Jack," he said.

"Call me Audrey," I said.

He patted my shoulder and said, "Thank you for your sweetness, Audrey, and I plan on enjoying the concert. I hope you have a lovely evening as well."

Soon the violin and cello began to play, and when dusk descended, I lay back on my blanket, closed my eyes, and let the music come to me.

The girl looked younger than Molly. I saw her when I got off the elevator. She seemed to be trying to get into the room across from mine the whole time I walked down the long hall to my room. As I got closer I saw she had dropped her purse on the floor beside her while she inserted her card and tried the door handle again and again. When I neared, she leaned her head on her door and said, "Oh, God."

I've been miserable myself. I felt like an intruder.

I wanted to get into my room as quickly as I could. But as I slipped my card into the slot, I heard her behind me trying her door again, once more in vain. I would rather have done anything than try to think of the right thing to say to the distraught woman. But I didn't have much of a choice. I had to do something. With an inaudible sigh, I took my card out of the slot and slipped it into my pocket.

"Miss," I said, walking over to stand next to her, "do you need help?"

"I can't even open my stupid door," she said, tears brimming in her eyes and slipping down her face.

"Could I try?"

She thrust her card at me.

When I slipped it into the slot, the tiny red light appeared.

"See!" she said.

"Maybe they gave you the wrong key," I said, looking at her envelope. I was thinking of asking if I could take it down to the lobby for her when I noticed the number on the envelope didn't match the door she was trying to open.

"Here's your problem," I said, patting her arm. "This is the wrong room. It looks like you're next door."

"Well, that figures!" she said, wiping the tears off her face with the back of her hand.

I thought about opening the correct door for her, I thought about asking her if she needed anything else—it even crossed my mind to ask if she wanted to come to my room and have a nightcap Coke with me. I assumed she was alone; she certainly looked alone, and I thought she needed to take a deep breath and calm down.

But before I had a chance to decide what to say, she jerked the card out of my hand, mumbled a thank-you, and hurried the few steps to the door that matched her card. I stood there for a minute after she entered her room, glad she had no further irritation, glad after all to go to my room alone. I was tired.

Tired or not, I lay awake for quite a while, worrying about the poor girl. Why hadn't I acted on my impulse? Couldn't I have said, *You seem upset. Will you let me buy you a Coke or something? I have a daughter about your age, you see.* What might have happened? Could God have loved her through me? Might I have entered that hallway at just that moment for that very reason?

I'm not the only one who needs to know that God is near.

eleven

August 29

"Okay, okay," Willa wrote. "Just so you come. Would it be too much to give me a day's notice? Whatever, I'm *so* excited! But I hear you. I will plan nothing except places for Ed and me to go so we can stay out of your way. You *so* owe me a visit, though. Can't wait!!!"

I wrote her back and said I'd give her at least one day's notice, maybe two.

"And you're right," I added. "I do owe you a visit."

I owe her more than that. Willa had not left me in my room, desperate and alone.

She had arrived at the house the day after Tom died. She grabbed first Molly and then Mark and hugged them ferociously, and then she looked around until she saw me sitting in my chair with my feet tucked underneath me. She came over and sat in front of me and rested her head against my protruding knees.

"I love you," she said.

Then she looked into my eyes, tears pooling in hers, and said, "I've come to help."

She and Rita stayed at the house answering the phone and receiving plants and flowers while Mark and Molly and I picked out a casket, took clothes to the funeral home, wrote an obituary, and planned the funeral. Looking back, I think when I completed the things I had to do, it began—"death in life."

Willa and Rita were there to help me and the kids, as far as I remember, every moment from the time they heard about Tom until the day after the funeral. Willa stayed almost a week longer, helping Mark with all the necessary paper work, running errands, helping me with thank-you notes.

"What else can I do?" she asked one morning after placing a plate of toast and a glass of orange juice in front of me. "You aren't ready to go through Tom's things, are you?"

"No, no, I'm not ready for that. The kids and I can do that later."

But although Mark and Molly have both taken several things that were especially dear to them, we have yet to go through his things. Tom would have laughed at that since I gave him no longer than one hour to read the morning newspaper before I had it in the recycling bin, or so the story goes. But it is not a joke that if I haven't used or worn something in a year, I find someone to give it to. Cleaning out my things when I'm gone should take Mark and Molly thirty minutes.

But Tom's things remain. Not in an attempt to cling or to deny, although I do dread his things not being there. I have simply never found the energy or desire to complete the task competently. And this is a task that I must do, no one else.

After the kids left, Willa spent a few days alternating between trying to feed me and trying to get a real smile out of me, or any sign of life. I thanked her for her help and for loving me so completely, and then I told her to go home to Ed. In the last ten days, she had seen him only the day of the funeral.

"I will if you promise to come see us later this summer," she said.

"I'll see."

But I didn't, and now I understand why she pressed me, why she didn't trust the "I'll see" I wrote earlier this week. She, like my children, deserves better.

I'm trying.

⌒

Today I explored the Wildcat Bluff Nature Center. Not too far from downtown Amarillo, it is advertised as an opportunity to imagine a different time.

That sounded good.

The fact that Wildcat Bluff was aptly named by early cowboys for a den of wildcats that lived under the bluff gave me some pause, but nothing in the literature suggested

I might run into one as I walked the trails that threaded through six hundred acres of rolling grasslands. Though the material suggested these acres were inhabited by many interesting creatures, I figured at best I'd run into a horned lizard.

With two bottles of water, an apple, and some granola bars stuffed in my canvas purse (it's become my version of a backpack), I put on my straw hat and sunglasses and started down the trails. I wasn't the only person there by any means, but at times it seemed like I was. I heard distant voices often enough to comfort me, but much of the time I had the prairie to myself. I had stopped to drink half of one of my bottles of water, thinking how delighted I was that I had not run into a rattlesnake or horned toad, when I heard a loud, cackling call and saw a striped creature—two feet long, head low, long tail—zip across the road. I think I actually giggled, I was so surprised. I had just seen a roadrunner. Maybe he'd come from a late, lingering lunch and that's why I hadn't seen a lizard or a snake.

If that weren't enough, not long before I decided to turn back, I found a place that could almost be called shade and sat down to relax and eat a snack. I was thinking about that roadrunner, wishing he'd zip by again, when I noticed a couple of critters a few yards off the trail nibbling on grass. They took turns looking at me, but after a while, since I sat quietly, hardly making a move, they didn't seem the least bothered about me. I was snacking with prairie dogs! At least, *near* them. Though they are supposed to be kin to the squirrels that visit my backyard and ravage my bird feeders, the chunky little things seemed much more interesting, much more adorable. As I watched, one scampered away into the grasses, but the other one sat on his haunches by his burrow and kept an eye on me. I gazed at him, and he gazed at me. I really couldn't believe I was sitting there making eye contact with a prairie dog. I don't know how long we sat staring at each other, but quite a while, until voices on the trail dispersed the magic and my friend disappeared into his underground home.

This journal is the only snapshot I have of that prairie dog, but it's a pretty good likeness, if I do say so myself.

Later, after I ate dinner and took a long shower, I sat on my bed, my back against four pillows and a headboard, and turned to the last section of John 6. With the Bible open on my lap, I took time before I read to close my eyes and thank God for the gifts of this day. So my heart hurt when I opened my eyes and read what Jesus says when so many turn away because of his "hard teaching."

"You do not want to leave too, do you?" Jesus asks them.

Simon Peter says: "Lord, to whom shall we go? You have the words of eternal life."

After I put my Bible on the nightstand, I prayed a short prayer: "I, like Peter, don't want to leave you, Lord." Then I got dramatic on the creator of the universe and prayed his words back to him: "*I* am with *you* always."

Though it seems inconceivable at times, I think that matters to him.

August 30

I arrived in Santa Fe this afternoon, and for the first time I walked into a hotel and couldn't get a room, which is amazing considering how seldom I book ahead. Tom would never arrive at a destination without a reservation, but I've done it almost everywhere I've gone. And I doubt I'll reform, because there are several wonderful places to stay on or near the plaza, and I got a great room in the second hotel I tried. It was too late to do much when I got settled, but I strolled along the plaza and found a cafe, opened "since 1918." It looked like a place where I could get something good to eat to take back to my room. While I waited for one of the best quesadillas I've ever had, I took in the ambiance of the checked floor and steel-banded tables and the chatter of happy customers. In less time than I expected, a young man with black hair and blacker eyes handed me a to-go sack, and I left the gathering of locals and tourists, still preferring the privacy of my room when I eat alone.

After I returned to the room, I made an ice run and saw two teenagers, maybe thirteen or fourteen, trying to get a dollar bill into the Coke machine. In the time I stood there, they put it in three times, and three times the machine spit it back out.

"Here," I said, pulling a crisp dollar out of my billfold, "trade me. Maybe this will work."

"Thanks," one of the boys said, handing me his wilted one.

"Did you do anything fun today?" I asked while my dollar slid into the slot without incident.

"We rode horses," my beneficiary said, punching the Coke button.

They looked more like the four-wheeler type.

"It was great," the other boy said. "We saw a place in the distance where they make a lot of Western movies."

"*Young Guns*," the first boy said, taking a drink from his Coke. "And *Tombstone*. The guide said Billy Crystal made a movie there too."

"*City Slickers*?" I asked.

"That's it," he said. And then with one more thank-you they were off, leaving me to fill my ice bucket and wrangle the Coke machine alone.

I can't say what I might do while I'm here, but I will not be horseback riding anywhere. I'd go to a zoo first. That movie set surely wouldn't get me on a horse. Nothing would. I made that mistake once, twenty years ago, visiting my brother in Kentucky.

Our son, Mark, had been ten or so, the perfect age, Henry said, to go horseback riding in the hill country. He made arrangements with a local stable for a two-hour ride and generously paid for the five of us. My brother, my husband, and my two children rode in front of me like seasoned cowpokes. Looking at them made me happy, and I enjoyed the ride—for maybe fifteen minutes.

One of the guides stayed back, riding behind me the whole time, trying to get my horse to quit eating grass. When my mare eventually and grudgingly gave it up, she tortured me by *tharump, tharump*ing to catch up with the others, while the guide yelled at me to keep my heels down even though doing so broke both of my knees, the frosting on my miserable cake. One of the happiest moments of my life was looking up to see the roof of the horse barn. When we finally rode up to the corral, it took both Tom and Henry to pry my legs off the horse and lower me to the ground. Tom and the kids couldn't conceal their involuntary smiles. I faux glared at Tom.

"Henry, whatever you paid for my time on Sasha," I said, stumbling to the car, "it was too much."

The boys at the pop machine were lucky I didn't go into it. They were lucky I talked at all. I wasn't feeling as sociable as I had sounded when I came to their aid.

My drive to Santa Fe left me ready to hibernate in my room for at least a day or two. I blame the radio. I listened to it as I drove, selecting first one news station and then another. Eventually I found two music stations, Christian Pop and Broadway Show Tunes, and alternated between them. The Broadway station had just started playing the soundtrack from *West Side Story* when I returned to it the third time.

"Would you like me to get tickets to *West Side Story*?" Tom had asked one morning during our first full summer together.

"I don't think so," I said.

He looked up from the newspaper. The question had been rhetorical.

This was the day I told him that the fall of my senior

year I sang and played the role of Maria in our high school production of *West Side Story*. By this time Tom had heard me sing solos at weddings and church, and I had joined an all-city chorale that spring, but this was the first he'd heard about my starring role in a musical.

"Our high school plays and musicals were quite good," I said. "We did *The Sound of Music* when I was a junior."

"Really!"

"Actually, if you want the truth, I was a star."

He laughed. "I'll bet you were," he said. "I wish I could have been there."

Tom and I saw *The Sound of Music* together several years later, but we never saw *West Side Story*.

It belonged to a past I tried hard not to revisit, not because singing the score wasn't exhilarating, but because my relationship with Andrew began on the first day of rehearsals, and the experience of that musical nurtured it. Unlike most of the cast, Andrew had never been in choir and no one but members of his church even knew he could sing, but he auditioned for and snagged the role of Tony. We were Romeo and Juliet, members of feuding families singing and dancing toward tragedy in New York City. We had a chemistry I had only sensed when he looked back at me with such intensity six months before in Mrs. Henry's language arts class.

Kissing Andrew for the first time, on stage, in front of the cast, was memorable, but no more so than singing the duet "Tonight." The school newspaper said we were meant to sing together. The duet "One Hand, One Heart" is a beautiful prayer of commitment, but "Tonight" was the duet we enjoyed most and the song that was most responsible for bringing crowds to their feet at the end of each night's performance—another newspaper observation. I have enjoyed few things more than the hours of rehearsal and the six performances for that musical, especially singing words that both Andrew and I were experiencing as we, like Tony and Maria, began to fall in love. The lyrics and melody of "Tonight" combine to project the eagerness and passion Maria and Tony felt contemplating an evening together: "Today, the minutes seem like hours, the hours go so slowly, but still the sky is light. Oh, moon, grow bright and make this endless day endless night—tonight."

Andrew and I felt the same anticipation each time we waited to be together. I have never experienced anything remotely like it except for the night I dressed for dinner and waited for Tom Eaton to pick me up for our first date.

I really can't believe I didn't turn off the radio when I realized which Broadway musical was being featured. Instead I ended up listening to the whole score of *West Side Story* . . . and remembered a time Andrew and I had performed it with such passion.

twelve

August 31

I opened my laptop again to see if I had a reply from the kids. What I found was a one-sentence message from Andrew.

"Do you remember the night Willa climbed on top of that car?"

I can't think of another thing he could have written that would have made me laugh.

The summer after our senior year, a group of us spent at least one night a week at the drive-in. Sometimes we parked next to one another and sat on blankets or lawn chairs, sometimes we backed up Charles Monroe's pickup and sat in the bed to watch the movie. Other times the girls sat on the hood and leaned against the windshield of Laura Bradshaw's finned Dodge and the boys stretched out on top, because dents were indigenous to that old clunker, and Laura always said, "Pile on, the more the merrier."

The incident Andrew mentioned in his e-mail happened the night we took Mr. Ackerman's car to the drive-in because Andrew's was in the shop. We parked it four cars down from Willa and Billy Houser, her then-boyfriend, and another couple who had come with them, and we walked down to talk to them before the movie started. When music blared through the metal speakers and a picture flashed onto the screen, brilliant against the black sky, Andrew started pulling me back to our car, and I informed Willa where we were parked and told her she should come see us between the two features.

The first of the two movies was a horror film, something I typically avoided, and Willa got it in her head to sneak down to our car when the film got intense, climb on the trunk, crawl over the top, and drop her face down onto the windshield in front of us. She hoped to get a scream out of me and maybe even Andrew. Her plan worked perfectly except for the fact that when she slid her contorted face over the top and looked through the windshield, she didn't see our startled faces but the faces of a middle-aged couple parked next to us in a car very much like Andrew's. There was some satisfaction in the fact that the woman screamed. We looked over and saw Willa sliding off the car, apologizing, and pointing at us as some sort of explanation.

Yes, I remember that.

I didn't manage to delete everything from my memory.

I remember singing a duet arrangement of "O Holy Night" our first Christmas as a couple, for his congregation and then for mine. I remember being elected prom king and queen and dancing to "Tonight," played in our honor. I remember both of us working at an amusement park for two summers, hoping we'd have the same break time, loitering by each other's workstations if we didn't. I remember his helping me through math my first semester of college and my drilling him endlessly before history tests. I remember our dressing up in anything orange and heading to the stadium or the gym for Bedlam, any OSU and OU confrontation. And though I hate even to write it, I remember lounging in his car in front of my parents' house on summer nights or snuggling on the couch in my apartment when winter drove us inside, wondering how much longer I could wait to be Andrew's wife.

I remember these things and more. But I didn't tell Andrew. I didn't reply to him at all.

I have better things to do. When I return to my room tonight, I will have gone to Taos and back.

❧

As it turned out, I've been to the Twilight Zone and back.

I should have used a credit card to fill my car with gas instead of paying inside. But I needed a Diet Coke; plus I had an inexplicable yearning for CornNuts. Chances are I would have been spared my brush with death if I could have found the ridiculous things. I searched in every logical place for them before studying paper product and detergent aisles. Back in the snack aisle one more time and still thwarted, I was just about to ask one of the clerks behind the counter where they had hidden the CornNuts when the guy came rushing in from the darkness. I didn't notice his gun. I was trying to process the fact that he was wearing a canary yellow and cobalt blue ski mask in August.

"Get over here, lady," he yelled.

I stood halfway down the snack aisle and stared at him. Was he talking to me?

I saw the gun when he pointed it at me. "I said get up here. And you," he said, turning to point the gun at the young girl behind the counter, "you get over here too."

He seemed to know what he wanted, but his eyes lacked focus, and his mannerisms were erratic. I've never done drugs even though I came of age in the '60s, but this guy seemed under the influence of something serious. What, I couldn't guess. Thousands of hours of television viewing told me this was not a good scenario. If this were a segment of *Law and Order*, it would turn out badly for everyone involved.

The girl came around the counter and hurried toward me, crying. I must have looked dependable because she grabbed my arm and hid behind me.

"You," he said, pointing at the woman behind the counter, "get the money out of those cash registers and put it in a sack."

I haven't quite decided whether she was brave or stupid

when she reached for something under the counter. Ski Mask shouted at her, and I watched in disbelief as he aimed his gun and fired. Surely this was one of my dreams and Tom would whip off the mask and show me he was armed with only our grandson's cap gun. *See,* he might say, *you're not really in danger.* But those were not Tom's calm eyes, and the bullet that had punctured the back wall was real.

"Do it now!" Ski Mask screamed.

Having just experienced a bullet zinging over her head, the woman began pulling bills out of the cash register nearest her faster than fingers can normally move, lifting the tray out to gather the larger bills stored underneath it without being asked.

"You two get down," he said, turning back to us. The girl was crying harder now.

"Shhh," I whispered, "we'll be okay."

Our assailant pointed his gun at the girl and then at me. "Both of you shut up!"

It was while sitting on the dirty floor of the convenience store with my arm around a girl barely old enough to have a driver's license that I saw rows of CornNuts clipped on a rounder two feet from my face. I almost laughed. I suppose that means I'm crazy.

When the woman emptied both registers and handed Ski Mask the sack, he told her to get around the counter and sit with us. Then with us huddled there together, he shot over us one more time and ran out the door. We kept our heads down until we heard the door close, which is why we missed the pleasure of seeing the man run into two policemen heading into the store from a patrol car parked just out of view. They had him subdued before he could shoot over or at them. The three of us got ourselves up off the floor and walked outside to see that they had already cuffed the thief and pushed him into the back of their police car. He no longer wore a ski mask, but I couldn't make out his features through the car window. I didn't try very hard, even though it occurred to me I should go over and thank him for putting those bullets in the wall instead of us.

I opened the door for the other women instead, and as we reentered the store, I asked the older woman if she had sounded the alarm.

"No, but I 'bout got blown away trying. Those officers come in around this time several times a week, though. Good timing, huh? They're gettin' free coffee for a week!"

I felt like chipping in some CornNuts.

So there I was, giving a policeman my name and cell phone number, glad I wasn't being carted off to the hospital or the morgue. When they took Ski Mask away, I purchased my Diet Coke and CornNuts, told the ladies I was glad they were okay, and rushed back to the hotel. As I drove through the streets of Santa Fe, walked down a colorful, brightly lit hallway, and finally locked myself in my clean and quiet room, one thought dominated all others: A desperate man wearing a ski mask and pointing a gun at my face could have killed all three of us just as easily as he had fired warning shots over our heads. Looking at that gun so menacingly close to my face provided me great clarity. I knew I wanted to live. I want to get to San Diego by way of the Grand Canyon and Phoenix; I even want to go on up the California coast to Monterey and San Francisco, places I had told Tom I want to visit someday; and then I want to get home to my children and their sweet children.

Though I was, and am, shaken (Hello—I *was* a victim of an armed robbery!), somehow this has not made a bigger coward of me. I have not thought even fleetingly of turning back, of cutting this trip short. Sounding like Tom, I have explained to myself that I will have to purchase gas and Diet Coke in Springfield too, and I doubt I will be safer there than I will be anywhere else. Besides, statistics should be in my favor. What are the chances I'll ever be involved in another robbery? (My cynical side just whined, "Odds are seldom in your favor.")

I'm learning to accept that there are no guarantees. But I'm also acknowledging there really *are* wonderful opportunities. Right up until I sat on a dirty floor looking into the barrel of a gun, I had enjoyed this day immensely. I left my room around noon and spent the day following the Rio Grande from Santa Fe to Taos and back again. I stopped at a seven-hundred-year-old pueblo and paid the fee to take a fifteen-minute walk to see Nambe Falls. The gorgeous double drop waterfall thrilled me. I sat and stared at the tumbling water for quite some time. In a shop on the Taos plaza, I bought something to eat and had a solitary picnic at a stunning stretch of river, mysteriously unmarked by a scenic view sign (some state official's unfortunate oversight). I loved the Rio Grande and the drive between Santa Fe and Taos.

My mistake was stopping at a convenience store near the city limits of Santa Fe moments before an armed robbery was to begin.

When I made it back to this room tonight, I collapsed on the bed. I had no energy for removing my makeup or my clothes. I did pull back the covers so I could hide beneath them.

Before I fell into a merciful, restorative sleep, my promise came to comfort me: *"I am with you always."*

"I know," I whispered, "but I wish you could hold me."

The truth is, though, as sleep came like a gift, I did not feel alone.

September 1

Well, I've lived to see the first day of September. After yesterday, that suddenly seems quite remarkable.

I awoke this morning to sun peeking through a slit between the curtains. I had closed them last night after I woke up wondering why I had gone to bed with my clothes on. I got up, put on a gown, took off what was left of my makeup, and wrote the second half of yesterday's entry. I was back in bed pretty quickly, counting my sheep: "I will fear no evil, for you are with me"; "It is I; don't be afraid"; "I am with you always"; "I will never leave you nor forsake you."

I managed to fall asleep again, but dreaming made it fitful. Surprisingly, I didn't dream about crazed killers wearing colorful ski masks. Instead I dreamed of Tom. In fact, he made an appearance in two of the dreams. Tom used to say he never dreamed, or if he did, he never remembered a dream when he awoke. I can't imagine such a thing.

In the first dream I was stuck up to my armpits in something like quicksand. I saw Tom standing nearby on solid ground and called out to him.

"Tom, help me!"

"Hurry up," he said. "The kids are waiting for you in the Alamo."

"But, Tom, I can't move! Get me out of here!"

"You can get out of there, Audrey."

He had some nerve. I couldn't even lift my arms out of the muck.

"Thomas Hanes Eaton," I commanded, "get something and get me out of here!"

"The kids are waiting," he said.

I looked down, surprised to see that the mire I was caught in was now only up to my waist. I woke up, wondering if I ever managed to get out.

The other dream about Tom was equally as frustrating in a different way. He was sitting by the river where I ate lunch yesterday. When I walked up and saw him there, I was elated.

"Tom," I said, sitting beside him, smoothing my jean skirt underneath me, "where have you been?"

"At the waterfall," he said.

"I was just there!" I said. "Isn't it pretty?"

"Very pretty." Then he stood up and stretched. "Well, I'd better get going."

"What do you mean? I just got here."

"I have to go mow the yard."

"No, no," I said, grabbing his arm. "Stay awhile."

"I have to get it done, honey."

"Okay," I said, starting to get up, "I'll go with you."

"No," he said, "stay here and swim."

I looked down and saw I had on my bathing suit instead of a jean skirt and white T-shirt. And I noticed Helen, poppy red hair blazing in the sun, sitting beside me, throwing rocks into the river.

"Helen," I said, "what are you doing here?"

She smiled as if I had asked an amusing question.

When I turned back around, Tom was hardly discernible in a distant field, mowing on a John Deere tractor, much too far away for him to hear me calling, "Wait! Wait!"

I heard giggles then and turned to see Helen playing in a waterfall with Kelsie and Jada. They called to me, and I was thinking of joining them when I awoke.

Each time I dream of Tom, I recall Milton's sonnet about his late wife: "But O, as to embrace me she inclined, / I waked, she fled, and day brought back my night."

⌒

I finally left the haven of my room and spent the entire afternoon strolling down Canyon Road, where there were lots of people. Today daylight and people were priorities. Galleries and restaurants housed in adobes lined the streets, one after another, so many of them. Some of the galleries looked quite modern, with whitewashed walls and sparse displays. Art was displayed outdoors as well, and flower and sculpture gardens delighted me when I happened onto them. I enjoyed the paintings, sculptures, pottery, and other types of arts, but everything was pricey, and it's a good thing my cottage-style home isn't right for most of it.

But I did enter one shop that displayed paintings I could imagine in my home. As I entered, I stood aside for a couple hauling a large wrapped painting to their SUV; when they left, I practically had the place to myself, for a while anyway.

"If I can help you with anything, let me know," a woman said from behind an easel as I ambled through a spacious room where she was working in a corner, natural light pouring through a bank of windows beside her.

"I love the paintings," I said. "They're different from most of the things I've seen today."

"I'm glad you like them," she said. Her hair was pulled back in a chignon, and her long, full dress mimicked the muted colors of the paintings, a beautiful palette I've seen on the facades of old buildings in Rome and Venice.

She wiped her hands on a rag and put down her brush, and I realized I was talking with the artist.

She had captured scenes of New Mexico magnificently—the deserts, the river, the pueblos, the old churches, Canyon Road, the flower and sculpture gardens.

"Have you always lived here?" I asked.

"As a matter of fact, I haven't," she said. "Five years ago, my husband and I moved here from Chicago."

"You pulled a Georgia O'Keeffe?"

"I doubt either of us will live to be ninety-eight," she said, "but we did visit here and fall in love with it."

We talked for a while longer and walked together through two more rooms. She seemed to enjoy looking at her paintings as much as I did; I sensed they were old friends. We were standing before a large picture dominated by an iron railing with flowers spilling over it when I glanced over at a table where a small picture sat on an easel.

"Oh my," I said, walking over to stand before it. "That's lovely."

"It's one of my favorites," she said.

It had no price tag. I hoped the cost wasn't astronomical. That it was only an eight-by-ten made me think purchasing it might be a possibility.

I nodded to the painting. "I was there yesterday," I said. "Believe me, it was the nicest part of my day."

She smiled and I decided not to elaborate on my day except for the exceptional scenery.

"Nambe Falls is beautiful," I continued. "I wished as I stood looking at it—the water tumbling, the double drop, the landscape around it—that I could remember it forever, and here it is."

"I wanted to capture it," she said. "That's hardly possible, but I was satisfied."

We walked on through the rooms, talking about several more of her paintings, and I was honored that an artist whose work I admired was available to chat about her pieces on this first Friday afternoon in September. I left her shop with the picture wrapped and bagged, as excited as I've ever been about any purchase.

I saw the artist, Mona is her name, and her husband that evening at the Georgia O'Keeffe Museum and spoke to them as music played in the courtyard. I told her I hadn't seen a painting in the museum that I loved any more than the one I purchased from her that afternoon.

She laughed as though the idea were absurd, but she seemed pleased nonetheless. She gave me her card and said I should e-mail her sometime and stop in when I'm in the area again.

When I got back to the hotel, I unwrapped my waterfall and thought of the words in John 7 that I had read before I left this morning: "If anyone is thirsty, let him come to me and drink. Whoever believes in me, as the Scripture has said, streams of living water will flow from within him."

I feel like I'm standing in that waterfall, arms extended, palms up, like my Indian brave.

thirteen

September 2

The drive to Albuquerque didn't take long. This is Labor Day weekend, so I actually called ahead and booked a room. Tom and I never made it to Santa Fe, but we spent the night here on several trips we made to California, and for that reason alone I'm glad to be here. I had to smile as I pulled up to a gas pump and remembered the time we stopped here only to fill up and trade drivers on our marathon trip from California to Springfield.

On one trip west with the kids, we arrived in Albuquerque early enough to give in to the kids' pleas and take them to the water park. It is quite a nice one, with enough slides to have amused the kids and their dad.

They had rushed back and forth between the slides and the wave pool, stopping by to see me floating on the lazy river in my yellow inner tube. I like lazy rivers, the gentle rocking as close to the comfort of being in the womb as I can imagine. I might have set a record for laps that day, coming out only for a drink and a forced trip to the slide area to watch my family zip down all seven slides. Actually, I enjoyed watching them; it was their nagging that bugged me.

"Come on, Mom, try it!"

Even Tom urged me to do what I had no intention of doing. I didn't parasail in Florida either, but sat on the beach, watching them soar through the air, later listening to them exclaim about the thrill of it.

"You really should try parasailing, Audrey," Tom said over a pile of French fries the evening they survived it.

"Why do you think a woman who won't go down a water park slide would jump up and *parasail*, Tom? Here's an idea: You should spend time lolling on a lazy river."

So I have no idea what got into me today when I put my things away, pulled on my bathing suit, tied a long sarong around my waist, and drove to that water park. I walked right past the lazy river and put my things in a locker and headed for the slides, planning to go down every one of them before I left, including the enclosed one, ominously called Lightning.

Despite the fact that I had recently survived a wild man wielding a gun, fear filled me as I looked up at the first slide. Just climbing the stairs higher and higher, children rushing past me for another go at it, raised my heart rate substantially. Standing at the top and looking down the three miles to the pool below, I might have walked back down the stairs if I hadn't turned and looked down at a skinny little boy behind me, hair sticking out all over his head, skin the color of tea steeped in the summer sun.

"Go, lady," he said, "you can do it!"

I looked into his confident blue eyes and then at the petite girl in charge. She smiled and told me to sit down, lie back, cross my ankles, and fold my hands over my heart.

Is that a comforting image?

But before I could answer my own question, I flew down the thing (I know for a fact that I was riding the air at one point), submerging into the waiting water fewer than thirty seconds after I had been hurled from the top. Having watched the kids and Tom through the years, I knew to yank on my bathing suit underwater until I was decent, and then I popped to the surface to find steps and the next slide. Before I got up the stairs though, the boy from the top of the slide torpedoed into the pool and, without bothering to adjust his swim trunks, splashed through the water to give me a high five.

"Are you going again?" he asked.

"Not on this one," I said.

Next thing I knew, he was padding along beside me, telling me the slide I was walking toward wasn't as fast as the one we had just gone down.

"It's fun, though," he said.

I could see I had a slide enthusiast on my hands. The boy, ten-year-old Jared, lives in Albuquerque and uses his season ticket to come to the water park several times a week. I think he was in a panic that the park would be closed after Labor Day. His mom and sisters were somewhere in the park suntanning, he said with some disdain as he escorted me to the next slide. He was to meet them later at locker 152.

After the fourth or fifth slide, I thought I should say something. "Jared, surely *someone* is waiting somewhere to play with you!"

Someone a tad closer to your age, I thought.

"My buddy had to leave," he said.

"What about your sisters?"

"Nah, you're a lot more fun."

Hearing that sad news, I didn't feel the need to meet his sisters.

Jared and I went down all seven slides, saving Lightning for last—his favorite, and as it turned out, mine as well. When we finished the marathon, I decided a few laps around the lazy river might revive me enough to make it back to the hotel unassisted.

"So," I said, "what time are you supposed to meet your mother and sisters?"

"Five thirty," he said.

I looked at the waterproof watch I had worn, surprised it still worked. "It's quarter to six, buddy."

"Whoa!" he exclaimed and zoomed off, a horizontal bottle rocket aimed for a bank of lockers.

I was wrestling my inner tube into the lazy river when he walked by with a woman and two teenage girls. He hollered something at me and waved, all he could manage as they yanked him by his Superman T-shirt and herded him toward the exit.

The first thing I did when I got back to the hotel was e-mail the kids and tell them about my adventure. "I wish I could tell your dad," I wrote. "He'd say, 'Good going, Audrey!'"

"Stay here and swim," Tom had said in that awful dream, and it seems I took him up on it.

September 3

Before church this morning, I turned to John 8, where Tom had marked verses that record Jesus saving the adulterous woman from her accusers and then saying to her, "Go now and leave your life of sin." Such passages were among Tom's favorites. He used to say Jesus is in the forgiving business. There was no theme he loved to teach more than God's forgiveness. Because of that, my husband was a peacemaker in our church and in the school he oversaw. "Seventy times seven" wasn't an incredulous number to him; it was love's concession.

I've always thought I was quite good at forgiving, that in any lesson Tom taught on forgiveness, I was not student but merely moral support, if not prime example.

So I was as surprised as I was irritated when I got Andrew's latest message this evening.

"Are you ever going to forgive me?"

Several one-line replies came to me:

Who did you say you are?

What a stupid question!

Choices have consequences.

Get a life, Andrew.

On the twelfth of Never.

I have no desire to answer him. If I did, however, and if I let the Holy Spirit work in my heart first, I would likely say: *Don't be silly, Andrew, I forgave you long ago.*

And I did forgive him long ago. That I can't pinpoint when doesn't mean I didn't.

I once heard a speaker say that cutting someone out of your life is the same as killing the person. While I thought that a gross overstatement, Tom seemed to understand the premise. I wonder what he would say about my refusal to acknowledge Andrew's e-mails. I wouldn't know. We didn't discuss Andrew. Tom knew he broke up with me and that I left Oklahoma because of it. But only a year before we met, Tom himself had broken up with a girl he had dated almost two years.

So it goes.

But that was different, slightly more mutual, and she had some inkling it was coming. That would have to help. The summer after our freshman year at OSU, Andrew laid out our future: become engaged the summer after our sophomore year, get married the next summer, complete our last year of undergraduate work as man and wife in a cute little apartment. Then I'd teach and put him through law school, which would be followed by his brief but illustrious career as a lawyer before his inauguration as the youngest governor of the state of Oklahoma.

So I could not have been less prepared for what he did two months short of putting an engagement ring on my finger. If there were any signs, I didn't detect them, even in retrospect.

The night he ruined everything, my three roommates had made plans for the evening so Andrew and I could have an intimate dinner for two in the apartment. I had never cooked for him before, had never cooked a dinner by myself, period. I spent part of my spring break in Mom's kitchen learning the art of making her memorable meatballs, and back at the apartment, I made no fewer than three separate batches of spaghetti to make sure I didn't put a sticky mess on the table. The afternoon of the momentous dinner, I made a salad and stirred up the special Austin dressing passed down from my great-grandmother, and I made a from-scratch carrot cake, promising the girls I'd save them most of it. When preparations for dinner were under control, I put flowers in the middle of the yellow Formica table and went to my bedroom to prepare myself. I wanted to look as perfect as possible.

After a lengthy shower and a ridiculous amount of time working with my long, straight hair, I could have auditioned for and won a spot in a shampoo commercial. I slipped on a new sleeveless minidress with an empire waist and put on a pair of platform shoes, somehow fashionable at the time. I

lightly sprayed my whole body with Andrew's favorite perfume and stood before my mirror for an assessment. Observ-
ing myself from as many angles as possible, I had to admit
I had met my goal.

Then I went to my top dresser drawer and pulled out
the package I'd wrapped with such care the night before;
Mother had taught me how to tie an impressive bow during
my last trip home. Shopping with Willa at an antique mall
during spring break week, I had found a pewter circle with
filigree edging and the letter *A* in the center and snatched
it up, planning to have it made into a keychain for Andrew.
The jeweler had called me last week to say it was ready, and
when he opened the box for my inspection, I told him it was
perfect. I couldn't wait to give it to Andrew. A gift for no
reason, extravagant according to Willa, seemed the greatest pleasure to me, a woman filled to the brim with love for
Andrew Ackerman.

When he walked in, he told me I looked beautiful. He
had been saying that for almost three years, but this night
he spun me around to get the full effect of my dress and
shoes, and he pulled my hair back in his hands, forming a
long ponytail, and buried his face in my neck. He seemed to
be memorizing me. I suppose *that* might have been a sign; I
interpreted it as delight. I took him into the kitchen, which
was so tidy one would think I'd had the meal catered, and
he ate like it was his first meal of the day and complimented
everything from the main dish to the dessert. He seemed to
understand this evening was a gift of love.

"I have something for you," I said as I put the dessert plates in the sink.

When I came out of my bedroom with the little square package, he had left the kitchen table and was standing in the living room.

"I need to talk to you, Audrey," he said.

"Okay," I said, oblivious to his mood change, "but I want to give this to you first."

He took the small box from my hand and put it on the coffee table. "No, sit down with me for a minute."

Those words and the seriousness with which he spoke them, and his eyes, mysteriously apprehensive, finally penetrated my bliss. He was suddenly as removed as he was serious, and sitting beside him on the couch, I began to understand, however inconceivable the thought, that this talk was going to be about us, the couple, and it would not be a good one.

How he said what he said, I cannot remember. He stammered something about our being too young to become engaged. I think he said we should see other people before making such a big decision.

"What in the world are you talking about?"

He seemed frustrated with the inadequacy of his words and blurted out, "I just think we should break up for a while."

I thought of a bumper sticker we had seen and laughed at. Something about setting people free, and if they're really yours, they'll come back to you.

"Andrew," I said as calmly as I could, "don't do this to

us. Don't throw away what we have, what we are. Don't. Please don't."

I put my hands on each side of his face and looked into the blue eyes I had loved for so long and said the useless words again: "Don't do this."

He took my hands away from his face, put them in my lap, and studied the door behind me. I comprehended in that moment, though I was barely twenty years old, that when someone makes the decision to disconnect, even if that someone is Andrew, words are powerless to prevent it.

I began to cry, to sob really, and perhaps from pure instinct, he held me. He kissed my hair. He rocked me in his arms. But when I could stop crying, he untangled himself from me.

"I should go," he said.

"Go? Look at me, Andrew."

He did me the courtesy, and his pain too was palpable. I wiped any tears left on my face with my hands, hating how I must look now.

"I don't know who she is," I said, "but I hope she's worth what this will cost us."

He got up and walked to the door.

I stood too, trying to breathe, and noticed the present I had wanted so badly to give him sitting foolishly on the table where Andrew had placed it. He was on the porch, the door open between us, when I called out to him one last time.

"Andrew! Take this," I said, walking across the threshold and shoving the box into his hand. "It's a going-away present."

Then I turned and walked into the house, shut the door, leaned against it, and tried to fathom his unfathomable last words: "I should go."

During the last six weeks of school, I ran into Andrew on campus on two separate occasions, walking hand in hand with the governor's daughter, and decided I had an answer for the Bee Gees' question, "How Can You Mend a Broken Heart?" I told Willa no more running into Andrew; I was going to live with my aunt in Missouri and would finish my teaching degree there. She understood. She had been with me the second time I saw Andrew and his new girlfriend across the lawn, had stood beside me after they had turned a corner and disappeared from view, had heard the groan emerge involuntarily from somewhere deep inside of me, from a place in the human heart we didn't even know existed. Instead of reaching out to me, she had stood back, awed by the manifestation of such raw grief.

But none of that has mattered for a very long time now.

After church today I rode the world's longest tram and toured another Old Town, collecting them, it seems.

It was a nice Sunday until I opened Andrew's message.

Willa wrote too: "Where are you?!!!"

Bless her.

fourteen

September 4

I arrived at the Grand Canyon earlier this evening and got a room at a lodge inside the park. It's rustic, as it should be, I suppose, but comfortable and close to the shuttle buses that will take me everywhere I want to go. There was enough time after I arrived for me to take the blue shuttle to Yaki Point. I think it was at this very spot I argued with Tom and the kids about flying low by one of the natural wonders of the world.

"We've been here all morning!" Mark said.

"We've been at *this* observation point for five minutes!" I said.

They weren't Philistines. This was day thirteen of a two-week vacation, and they were ready to get home. Tom had made the side trip so we could at least take a look at the canyon we had heard so much about, but now, "time was a wastin'."

As the three of them rushed to the car, I turned and looked at the magnificent view one more time and made it a promise: "I'll be back."

"Here I am," I said this evening.

I'm sure the canyon was pleased.

I grabbed a sandwich on the way up to my room and ate it with Tom's Bible open on my lap to one of Jesus' "I am" statements: "I am the light of the world."

That made up my mind for me. Tomorrow at sunrise I am going to have a good spot at one of the observation points. I've heard sunrises over the Grand Canyon are spectacular, and I hoped it wouldn't be cloudy so that I could witness the full effect of its beauty and symbolism. I'm ready for it, and for the first time since Tom died, I set the alarm. And I set it for five fifteen!

On the road today, I couldn't help but think about Andrew's message. It had never occurred to me that I hadn't forgiven him. Some things eventually cease to matter, and forgiveness becomes a given. But thinking back on every encounter with Andrew since he walked out that door, I find nothing that suggests forgiveness.

He called me in September after I moved to Springfield to attend college and asked why I had done such a thing.

"Are you still dating Melissa?" I asked.

"Yes."

"Well, there you go," I said. "And, Andrew, I'm sure sorry if my leaving has made you feel bad."

He didn't say anything then, and neither did I. After a minute passed, both of us with nothing to say, I pushed the button to disconnect.

Over two years later, Andrew called me at my parents' house during Christmas break. He had broken up with Melissa that summer and had just returned from a fall internship in Washington and run into someone who told him I had come home wearing an engagement ring.

"Do you love him?" he asked.

"You know what, Andrew, the answer to that should be obvious, but even if it isn't, it's none of your business."

"I'm sorry you're still mad."

"I'm not mad; that was just a stupid question."

"Will you go get a Coke with me?"

"I'm engaged, Andrew. No, I won't go get a Coke with you. I have to go."

"Merry Christmas, Audrey."

Before I could decide whether to return the holiday sentiment, he hung up.

Seven months later, he called me in Springfield when I got home from my wedding rehearsal. It upset me that my heart rate increased noticeably when I recognized his voice. He said he was in Springfield and would come by and get me if I wanted to change my mind about marrying someone besides him.

"That's not funny."

"I'm sorry. I know it isn't. And I know the timing is bad, Audrey, but I have one night left before you make the biggest mistake of your life, one night to tell you that I was a fool when I broke up with you. I wanted to tell you that when you were home for Christmas, but you wouldn't give me the chance. I've called your apartment I don't know how many times since then, but you're never home. I finally gave up and sent you a letter almost two weeks ago. It came back yesterday. I sent the darn thing to Springfield, Illinois, instead of Springfield, Missouri."

"It wouldn't have made any difference."

"I can't believe that. I love you, Audrey. I always have. I need you to know that."

I couldn't believe what I was hearing. Besides the fact that Andrew had apparently taken up residence in an alternate universe, I could not believe he would do something as crazy as calling me the night before my wedding. I couldn't believe he would make himself so vulnerable, that he could feel that desperate.

"Don't do this," he said, and the words took me back to my plea on the worst night of my life. I doubt he was aware of the irony.

"I'm as sure about this wedding as I've been about anything in my life. I can't wait until tomorrow. If you're really in Springfield, go home. I can tell you from experience, you'll get over this."

I didn't see him again until our tenth high school reunion. Early in the evening, he came up to me and Tom, eager it seemed to meet Tom and to introduce me to his wife, Susan, a lawyer in the Oklahoma City firm where he worked. Tom and I sat across the room from them at a table with Willa and Ed, and Jackie Harris, another OSU roommate, and her husband. I was irritated with myself for stealing more than one glance at Andrew, and inappropriately gratified that each time I did he was looking at me. Later that evening Tom asked Willa to dance, knowing she loved to dance and that Ed refused even to sway to the music. When they left the table together, I was startled to see Andrew walking toward our table and more than uneasy when he stood beside my chair and looked down at me, asking me to dance.

But I stood up and went with him to the dance floor.

"You are more beautiful than the girl I remember," he said with no other preamble.

For the first time in eight years, I looked into his eyes, my only response.

When I finally spoke, I had the perfect question: "Where's Susan?"

"She's tired," he said. "She went back to the hotel."

"You're not staying with your parents?"

"She prefers a hotel."

He pulled me closer, and I let him, choosing closeness over the discomfort of looking at him. We danced in silence for a minute or two, and I remembered "us."

I was relieved when he pulled back to look at me again. "Let's talk about you," he said.

"Oh, Andrew," I said with a sigh, "let's not. In fact, I'm going to go find my husband."

I walked off the dance floor before the music ended but turned to say one last thing, quite presumptuous of me as I think of it now. "Perhaps you should go find your wife."

Why was I so needlessly curt after so many years?

Intuitively, I must have thought Andrew posed a threat to me. For several years after Tom and I were married, Andrew crossed my mind from time to time, and each time it happened, I felt enormous guilt. Eventually, when his name surfaced in my consciousness for whatever reason (I quit trying to analyze it), I taught my heart to say, "There is no Andrew," until finally there wasn't. I suppose I was curt because I wanted to keep it that way. I considered my motives noble.

After the reunion, it was a nonissue. He had his life, and I had mine. Tom and I were in the second half of decade one. Things were good and getting better, and Andrew seldom entered my thoughts.

The only other time Andrew and I were together, I didn't know it. The occasion was my father's funeral, eight years ago. Andrew sent beautiful flowers and a card, and I asked Mom to write him a nice thank-you note, which Henry and I signed. Maybe as much as a year later, Willa asked me in the course of some conversation if I had seen Andrew at my father's funeral.

"Are you sure he was there?" I said. "His name wasn't in the guest register."

She was sure. She had seen him in the back row at the

service, and at the cemetery she had seen him standing by his car while everyone else gathered around the casket for a final prayer. Later, while friends and family greeted Mom, Henry, and me, she had looked in his direction a second time, thinking she would go speak to him, but he was gone.

~

I wrote Willa earlier this evening and told her I had just arrived at the Grand Canyon and that I'd probably be at her house Friday evening, but not to plan dinner for me, because I couldn't tell her what time I would arrive.

I wrote the kids an update, and I wrote Rita, checking in before she leaves on her trip and wanting to tell her the story of my trip to Yaki Point.

Then I wrote Andrew: "I'm fine. And I forgave you long ago."

September 5

There wasn't a cloud in sight this morning!

I arrived at the observation point while it was still dark and found a spot in front of the iron railing. I wasn't the first to arrive, and I was glad I could still find an unhindered view. Standing there, I found it fascinating that I was one of only a few English-speaking tourists. I identified at least four other languages, the most prevalent, Japanese and German. When the light that precedes the sun made an appearance, talking in any language ceased, everyone's eyes intent upon the horizon and what it had to say, rather than on those around them. Most people had brought cameras and video recorders, some setting them meticulously on tripods, but a few of us came with nothing except expectancy. We looked first at the ridge from where the sun would emerge any moment to the canyon walls on the opposite side, which the sun would soon illuminate. A heavy gilded curtain parting for the most venerated performance on the most impressive stage in the world could not have produced more anticipation. We longed for the sun to make its entrance, and when it did, we gasped, almost in unison.

I leaned against the rail, taking in nature's opulence, and whispered, "Magnificent Lord, thank you for this gift." Only a sense of social decorum kept me from lifting my arms to heaven and singing the chorus of "How Great Thou Art"!

As it was, a Chinese lady looked at me tentatively, as though she was sizing up my mental state. She seemed somewhat relieved, I think, when I said nothing else but merely smiled at her. That smile must have been something because it served to catapult me into a photography session. She asked me with amazingly effective hand motions and body language to take a picture of her and her husband and son, the canyon glorious behind them. It was my pleasure. And before I left the lookout point, I had snapped at least ten pictures of happy couples and families, and one of a lady from Germany, alone like I, who wanted a record of her being here. She seemed to sense I would understand that.

I watched her walk away and hoped sleepyhead friends were waiting for her back at a lodge. But even if they weren't, she'd seen a brilliant sunrise over the Grand Canyon.

When the sun was well into the sky, I went back to my room and made myself presentable before getting the car and driving out of the park to pick up a personal pan pizza. (I may enter myself in the *Guinness World Records* for most pizzas eaten on a road trip.) Ravenous, I ate in my room, wishing I'd picked up two pizzas since the one sitting in the box on my lap was the size of a bagel. But that was the only glitch in my morning, and I bowed my head over the tiny pizza and thanked God for my daily bread and for his handiwork and my opportunity to see it in such a way. Then I clicked on the television and watched a *Law and Order* rerun, which can be found almost anytime of the day or night. My firsthand experience with the "law" part had not stifled my interest in the show. I did, however, find myself dozing through a second episode and decided to pull back the comforter and take a serious nap. Five fifteen in the morning, I am not used to.

It seems like I had a passel of dreams, but when I opened my eyes, I could recall only the last one. I was floating in the lazy river when up ahead I saw a man lounging in his inner tube, moving it along, using his hands for paddles. He looked a lot like Tom from the back, his sandy hair shiny and charmingly disheveled. I rushed through the water, dragging my inner tube behind me until I got close enough to see his face, and I almost cried when I realized it really was Tom. I could see my reflection in his hazel eyes.

He smiled. "Look who's in the lazy river," he said.

"I thought you were golfing," I said, still amazed to find him there.

"This is great," he said, "especially the scenery."

I looked beyond him and saw the expanse of the Grand Canyon, but before I could take in its grandeur and wonder who thought to put a lazy river on the rim, I heard laughter behind me and turned to see the Chinese lady floating on her back without an inner tube, kicking her feet and propelling herself past Tom and me with a wave and a nod.

"Let me take a picture of you, Tom," I said after waving back at my sunrise friend, "with the canyon in the background."

He pulled himself out of the water and then helped me out while our inner tubes floated around the bend without us.

"No," he said, taking the camera from around my neck. "I'll take one of you."

He posed me in front of the barricade at Yaki Point.

"That's a good one," he said, looking into my eyes, smiling my favorite smile.

I was rushing over to see what he saw on the screen of my digital camera when I awoke.

Closing my eyes, I willed myself back to sleep, wanting to find Tom again. But he had vanished with the dream, and tears slid down my temples and dampened the edges of my hair.

For a moment, I wondered whether the dream was a blessing or a curse, but I wiped the tears away and got up and washed my face before reading another group of verses in John, the best remedy I could think of for the longing I suddenly felt and didn't know what to do with.

Jesus shows his understanding of human nature: "If you hold to my teaching, you are really my disciples. Then you will know the truth, and the truth will set you free." I have experienced that freedom many times in my life, but never any more poignantly than I have in these last weeks. I am being set free from "death in life"—today's dream has not changed that. I'm overwhelmed with wonder at the work God is doing in my life. To think I might have been among those who had "no room" for his Word.

I'm going to take a shuttle to watch the sunset from one of the points later, and then before I close my eyes on this day, I'll write the kids and tell them about this morning. Molly said in her last note that she thought this trip was good for me.

"But please tell me," she wrote, "that you *will* be home by Thanksgiving."

I imagine I'll be home long before that, Molly.

Lord willing, of course.

The creek rising, I'm not worried about.

fifteen

September 6

Dressed in khaki walking shorts, a white T-shirt, and hiking boots I bought yesterday, I set my canvas bag by a chair in the lobby and plopped down to study my Grand Canyon guide.

"Going on a hike?"

I looked up to see a stout woman on the couch across from me, her right foot resting on her left knee. She smiled.

I smiled back. "Yes," I said, "I'm going to try it."

"My sister and I hiked yesterday. Mercy, we didn't know if we were going to make it back to the top, but as you can plainly see, we did. That should encourage you. We're heading to the river today for some white-water rafting."

"Oh my," I said. "I hope your insurance is paid up."

She thought that was hilarious.

"No, I told you wrong. We're going on a *smooth* water raft trip. We didn't get reservations for the white-water rafting. Besides, the shortest one of those trips is three days! We waited too long for something like that. This one's a half-day trip, just about right for Pearl and myself. We'll be back from our trip by dinnertime."

She stopped for breath. "I'm Ruby," she said.

"I'm Audrey."

Ruby looked maybe fifteen years older than I, but a good deal friskier.

"I finally retired from the gas company last month," she said, tucking a piece of her short gray hair behind her ear, "and my sister Pearl and I decided it was time to see this place. She's upstairs getting our first-aid kit. She needed a Band-Aid, and I told her we might as well take the whole mess with us."

"Well, I've got new boots—"

"They *look* new," she said.

I doubt Ruby meant to interrupt—the observation simply erupted.

"So," I continued, "I've put a Band-Aid on every potential pressure point. There are so many Band-Aids on my feet, I think I should have bought boots a half size bigger."

Ruby thought that was hilarious too.

"Just let me tell you this. You and those boots better stay out of the way of any mules on that trail."

Ruby, of course, unacquainted with my history with horses, could not have known her warning was unnecessary.

Horses, mules, donkeys—they're all the same to me. Out of their way is where I always plan to be.

"Did you ride the mules down to the canyon floor?" I asked.

"You bet we did, the second day we were here, and it's an experience I could have lived without. Did you know that those mules have to rest, and just guess how they do that?"

She went on before I could guess.

"There's no room to do it in any sensible way. What they do is turn to face the edge. One false move, you're over the side and on a two-mile ride straight to the bottom."

"Two miles?"

"Something like that. Anyway, a young fellow in our group somehow came off his mule. I about had a heart attack, and I'm not kidding."

"What happened?"

"Girl, they had to send in a helicopter after him, and do you know what that costs?"

I couldn't imagine.

"Three thousand dollars! And I'm not kidding."

"Oh my, that probably ruined his morning," I said.

Ruby laughed again. It was pleasant being around someone who could laugh so readily.

"Well," she said, looking beyond me to the staircase, "here's Pearl! We'd best get going."

She stood up and called Pearl over. "You need to meet Pearl," she said.

"Are you two twins?" I asked after the introductions.

They laughed at that, though they must have heard it many times. Pearl has the same gray hair, cut short like her sister's, and she's only a tad stouter and taller than Ruby. Neither of them bothered with makeup, giving them a scrubbed, take-me-or-leave-me look, and both seem to enjoy life and each other immensely.

"Audrey," Ruby said, "why don't you eat dinner with Pearl and me in the dining room tonight? We can tell each other about our day. Two for the price of one."

I was sure they'd have plenty to tell me, but dinner with relative strangers in a dining room didn't have much appeal. I've grown comfortable eating alone in my room.

"Oh, I don't know, Ruby."

"Got other plans, huh?"

"No, not really. Okay, maybe I *will* come. You're nice to ask."

"Nice nothing," Pearl said, "she's desperate. She needs somebody besides me to talk to. She's heard all my stories more times than she can count."

"Six thirty," Ruby said, grabbing Pearl's arm and heading for the door.

I sat smiling and watching them until they had climbed into a waiting van, and then I returned to my canyon guide, trying to decide which trail to take for my first serious hike. I chose the trail that promised the best views for a short hike—relatively short anyway.

I have to say I made a good choice. I was exhausted when I climbed back on the shuttle several hours later. Probably

I should have started with a shorter trail, but the view *was* spectacular and I felt proud of myself for making it. So what if I did stop more often than any other person I saw on the trail?

I'm going to take a shower, read, and then I think I'll go down to the dining room for my first public meal since I left home.

⌐

"Well, don't you look pretty," Ruby said when I walked into the dining room and found the sisters.

I had traded my khaki shorts for a soft knit khaki skirt and added a brown knit tank top and a jean jacket. Ruby wore a navy dress with a boxy matching jacket, and Pearl wore a red cotton skirt and a cotton overblouse with a geometric design that used every color in a crayon box except the red of her skirt. I fully expected Stacy and Clinton from *What Not to Wear* to burst through the doors and whisk Pearl away. But I would have stopped them. The world needs its Pearls.

"Saved a chair for you," Pearl said.

"Guess what, ladies?" I said, pulling out my chair and sitting between them, completing the triangle at the intimate round table. "I didn't run into a mule today."

"Well, that's good," Ruby said. "We had a dandy day too. You might want to try the smooth water rafting trip. I'd have to say it was easier than that hike we took yesterday."

"You know, if I have time, I might. Tom and I used to canoe, and I enjoyed it so much."

After we placed our orders, I asked Ruby if she and Pearl had more family at home. She said she and her husband were never able to have children and that he died twenty-five years ago in a head-on collision with a truck that swerved into his lane. After all these years, Ruby winced and shook her head when she told me that. I think I did too.

"Pearl never married," Ruby continued with only the slightest pause, "but we have two brothers and two other sisters who have blessed us with lots of nieces and nephews."

When I asked if she and Pearl lived together, she said they had a duplex. "Works out good," she said.

She shocked me when she said they lived in Portland, Oregon. I wouldn't have guessed they were from the Northwest if they'd given me all night long and a thousand dollars to come up with where they were from. She explained that after her husband died, she and Pearl moved out from Fort Smith, Arkansas, to be near three of their four other siblings.

"Fort Smith isn't far from where I grew up," I said. "That seems brave, moving clear across the country at that point in your life."

"It wasn't as hard as you'd think. Pearl worked for JCPenney and they transferred her to a Portland store, and I got on at the gas company right away. We wanted to be around family. I guess we'll die there when the time comes."

"Probably so," said Pearl. "And that'll be all right. We don't have folks back in Arkansas anymore. And Oregon's pretty country too."

Ruby had ordered a fried chicken salad for an entrée,

which left her in charge of the conversation when the waiter brought Pearl and me our dinner salads.

"Our mother named us girls after gemstones, you see. Mama said that our names were likely as close to a gem as she was ever going to get. She also said it didn't matter none, because we were worth far more than any 'sparkly'—that's how she put it. Opal was first, then Pearl, me, and Onyx."

"Onyx," I said. "That's an interesting name."

"Yes, it is," said Ruby, "but not half as interesting as the boys' names."

"This is a good story," Pearl said, "and it's the honest truth."

"Mama decided to stay with an earth theme, so she named the boys Cotton and Wheat."

"Really," I said, opening a cellophane package of crackers. "I've heard of Cotton Mather, and I actually know a man in Springfield nicknamed Cotton, but I have never known, or even heard of, a Wheat."

"You haven't heard the punch line," Pearl said.

"Our last name is Fields," Ruby said.

"Okay," I said, putting down my fork. "You ladies are teasing me."

"No, we're not!" Ruby said. "Show her your driver's license, Pearl."

Pearl was already digging it out of her purse. She flipped open her billfold and there behind the plastic license cover was a picture of Pearl with the name Pearl Fields beside it.

"Cotton Fields?" I said.

"And Wheat Fields," said Ruby. "Mama didn't see a thing wrong with those names. Thought they sounded nice and honored practicality. Their names aren't up to Ima and Ura Pigg, I guess, but I love introducing my brothers, that's for sure.

"When Mama was forty years old, sitting at the dinner table with the six kids—we were pretty big by then—Daddy came in with a ring in his hand and laid it on the table in front of her. 'There,' he said, looking at each of us girls, 'there's you a diamond.' And sure enough, it was. It was a little one, but it was a diamond, and that was something, 'cause we didn't have much in those days. Mama put her apron up to her face and bawled like a baby.

" 'Goodness, Cleo,' Daddy said, 'I didn't buy it to upset you.' Mama put that ring on, right next to the thin gold-plated band he bought her the second year they were married, and she wore it all her days."

"That is a sweet story," I said.

"It really is," Ruby said. "I haven't thought about it in years. Have you, Pearl?"

"No, but here it is." She held up her hand, veined but soft and unusually smooth for her age, and I inspected the ring and its delicate setting. If they hadn't told me the precious diamond was there, I doubt I would have detected it.

"Opal was the oldest, so she was supposed to get it by rights when Mama passed, but all us girls decided Pearl should have it since she never married."

Pearl smiled.

"Another sweet story," I said.

They asked about me then, and over my tuxedo chicken, I told them about the kids and grandkids, told them Tom had died a year and a half ago, and told them I was on a trip to the West Coast to see what I could see.

"Well, honey, you sound like a brave one too," said Ruby.

Brave, did she say?

"And when you get to that coastal highway, you just turn your car north and get on up to Oregon. Pearl and I will show you the sights in Portland, and I'm not kidding."

I didn't think she was. Not for a minute.

September 7

I met Ruby and Pearl at ten for a late breakfast (late for them anyway). They were packed up and ready to check out but wanted to take a quick walk on the canyon rim before they started back to Oregon.

"A late breakfast is perfect," Ruby had said last night before we went our separate ways. "This way we won't have to eat but one other time tomorrow. I plan to put the pedal to the metal. Even with a late start I think we can make it home in two days."

"You sound like my husband," I said, "except he might try to make it in one."

Present tense lingers.

I ate a huge, delicious breakfast, enjoying the company and dreading the departure of Ruby Willingham and Pearl Fields. I walked with them to their car, and after they had hugged me good-bye and I had wished them a safe trip, Ruby pulled a notebook out of her purse and ripped a piece of paper out of it.

"Now, this has all the information you'll need when you get to Portland," she said. "You've got our phone numbers and our address with easy directions. If the Lord brings you up that way, and Pearl and I hope he does, you'd better call. You hear?"

"I hear you."

When the ladies got settled in the car, Ruby lowered her window and looked at me.

"This was a dandy trip," she said, "and you had a part in that, Audrey. You be careful when you head out of here tomorrow."

Tears pooled in her blue eyes. "Would you look at me," she said, starting the car. She backed out and took off without saying good-bye. She had said last night she didn't care for the word. The last thing I saw was Pearl leaning out of her window waving and shouting something about seeing me soon.

After they were out of sight, I began my day on the rim of the Grand Canyon. I planned to hike, hardly more than walk really, the rim of the red route, seven miles from beginning to end. This was a challenge, but I planned on taking the shuttle back, and I also knew I could catch it several places along the way if the seven miles became too much. But I wasn't running a race, I had all day if I wanted, and there were eight lookout points along the way, and places to stop and get my breath between points. The view at every point was awesome, a reflection of the God who provided it.

At a point about two miles into my hike, I found some shade and a place to plop for my first serious rest. As I sat there, a man and woman a little younger than I, along with a boy and girl who looked like they might be in their early teens, came from the trail into the open space of the observation point. The woman saw my shade and sat down not far from me while the man and the kids hurried down to the rail to take pictures.

"I wish I had your boots," she said.

I looked at the flip-flops she was wearing.

She held up one foot. "Not smart." She went on to say that they had intended to ride the shuttle to all the points, so her flip-flops hadn't seemed problematic. But at the last point, they'd decided they could walk the half mile to this one.

"I prefer flip-flops to boots myself," I said.

She retrieved a bottle of water from her purse and poured some on her arms and down the front of her. "It's steaming," she said.

Then she proceeded to tell me that she and her husband had brought their two oldest grandchildren to see the canyon. I told her she didn't look old enough to have teenage grandchildren, and she said that she had married young. "But," she added, "I had a good man, and we made it." She smiled at her husband, and he snapped her picture before turning back to pose the kids in a variety of spots in front of the railing.

"We've had fun with them, doing things we couldn't have done if we'd brought the younger kids. We took an overnight trip down to the canyon floor on mules when we first arrived. That was something."

"I have a friend who told me the mules rest facing the edge of the canyon," I said.

"That's true," the woman said, "but they have to rest, and if they do it facing the wall they can step back and fall over the edge backward. It happens. I was scared spitless sitting on my mule and looking over the edge, but my husband said he wanted the mules to know exactly what they were dealing with!"

Her husband, finished with picture taking, put his camera in its case, called the kids, and walked over with them to retrieve his wife. Taking her hands and pulling her to her feet, he told her it wasn't far to the next stop. She looked at me as though moving pained her.

"I might be able to make it if it's *real* close," she said. "Otherwise they can carry me."

"Good luck," I said.

I thought about those mules after she left. For fifteen months I'd "rested" facing the dull nothingness of the cliff, disregarding the potential for disaster. Better for me to overcome fear and dread instead, and face the edge of the canyon, where I can embrace beauty and avoid unnecessary catastrophe. It seems that's what I've finally chosen to do.

I stood and stretched, ready to walk the next section. It took me a total of four hours to get to Hermit's Rest. The bathroom and snack bar were a welcome sight. I stood in line to get an ice cream bar and saw a sign with Psalm 68:4 on it attached to a supporting beam. I was delighted someone had thought to place such perfect words at this spot. Knowing I probably wouldn't return here for a long time, I sat down and ate my ice cream slowly and looked out at the grandeur, wanting to somehow internalize it. I saw a huge bird soar by in the distance—an eagle, I think—but the way things have been going, I might have been given a glimpse of a rare condor. On the way to the shuttle, I stopped to throw away my wrapper and napkin and to read the psalm again.

I took a detour from John tonight and turned instead to Psalm 68:4. It seemed perfect to use as a benediction for my time at the Grand Canyon: "Sing to God, sing praise to his name, extol him who rides on the clouds—his name is the Lord—and rejoice before him."

Then, before I closed my Bible, my eyes moved down to the next verse, 68:5. I was stunned by the words waiting there for me: "A father to the fatherless, a defender of widows, is God in his holy dwelling."

I sat there with my Bible open on my lap for some time, knowing once more the "defender of widows" had tenderly reminded me that he was near.

sixteen

September 8

I rode a mule. And I'm not kidding, as Ruby would say.

It just worked out. I got up earlier than I would ever have wanted to and followed the smell of mules to the designated place of departure, where I learned there was a six-mile day trip to a plateau about fourteen hundred feet above the Colorado River.

"So," I said to the young man behind the counter, "do you have a spare mule I can ride this morning?"

"Sorry," he said, "we're full up."

"Hold it," his cohort said.

One of the girls in a family of six discussing the adventure they were about to share was apparently not at all up for it. As he spoke, I could hear the girl huddled with her family, being quite adamant about not killing herself on a fall to the bottom of the canyon.

I understood.

Never would I have dreamed I would have ended my time at the Grand Canyon descending it on the back of a mule.

"Tell me her name isn't Sasha," I said to Bart, the guide who helped me into the saddle of the smallest mule in the bunch.

"It's a he, ma'am."

Easy mistake.

"This isn't his first time out, is it?" I asked.

Bart actually smiled under his handlebar mustache. "No, ma'am. Ned here is as seasoned and as sure-footed as they come."

Okay then, I thought, reaching up to pat Ned after I got situated. "Good boy."

I'd bought a book of photographs depicting wonderful scenes of the canyon to put on the table next to my chair in the living room, but nothing could equal seeing it from the uncomfortable back of my mule, Ned. My favorite part of the experience was when he turned to rest facing the expanse of the canyon. It was terrifying and exhilarating.

Each time I thought about it on the way to Willa's, I smiled.

I don't think I was smiling when I thought about the e-mail I found from Andrew this morning.

"I was surprised to finally get a response," he wrote. "I'm glad to know you're okay and that you've forgiven me. I know

I'm pressing my luck here, but I would like to see you. I could make a trip to Springfield sometime if it's okay with you. Or if you're coming to see Willa one of these days, I could see you here. I've been thinking about this for a while and decided to at least ask—nothing ventured, nothing gained. What do you think?"

"I think you're crazy," I wrote.

Then, after my adventure on the mule and before I put away the laptop, I sent another message: "I'll be at Willa's tonight."

I arrived at Willa's around eight, just as Ed was pulling into the garage.

Willa ran out to meet me. "Woo hoo! You're here. I can't believe it!"

I got out of the car and gave her a hug. "I hope you don't mind—I've been snacking, but I didn't stop to eat dinner. You'll have to dig up something. I'm starving."

"No problem. I can't wait to feed you!"

We walked into the air-conditioned house, where Ed was putting groceries on the black granite counter.

"Hi, pretty lady," he said. "I'll get your bags and put them in the casita."

"Oh, thank you, Ed," I said as he walked back to the front door. "Lugging two or three suitcases and a laptop around has been the worst part of this trip. Tom usually had the trunk emptied and luggage inside our room before I could find my purse."

When Ed had closed the front door behind him, I told

Willa that most nights I leave my shoe bag in the car and simply get out the pair I think I'll need the next day.

"What about laundry?" she asked. "Your trip isn't hassle free, is it?"

"I send the laundry out, usually. And I'm getting used to the hassles. It hasn't been bad really. Overall, it's been good, in fact. Right now, however, everything I own needs washing or cleaning, so I hope you know what we're doing tomorrow."

She was ready to get my things and start the wash right then, but I told her I wanted nothing more than to sit down and let her chat away about her life.

She said she had a better idea.

"You get out to the casita and get settled. You'll find ice and Diet Coke in the refrigerator. Come back inside in a half hour and I'll have something for you to eat while I entertain you with my cheerful banter."

"I'm quite in the mood for your cheerful banter," I said, walking toward the door. "I'll be back."

When I came back into the house, Ed had gone off to join a card game at the clubhouse to give Willa and me time alone. While she talked, I ate a pasta salad she had put together while I unpacked and sorted laundry. Actually, we ended up entertaining each other. She caught me up on her kids and grandkids and I caught her up on mine, and when my hunger was satisfied, she wanted to know every place I had gone and everything I had seen and every person with whom I had talked or made eye contact, including the prairie dog. She thought I was making up Ruby and Pearl, and I said I'd like to know how I could make them up.

When we had given conversation a rest and were quietly cleaning the kitchen, Willa walked over to the desk.

"Listen to this," she said, pressing the message button on her answering machine. "Willa, this is Drew. Will you call me when Audrey arrives?"

"So," she said, "what's that all about?"

I told her about our e-mail exchanges.

"Well, that's interesting," she said. "You know, he didn't have a ring on the night I saw him at the restaurant. And he was with two other guys. It looked like a business dinner."

"You check out rings?" I asked.

"I was curious." She lifted my bare left hand. "I checked yours out too."

"An attempt to quit thinking of Tom in the present tense," I explained.

Willa gave me a quick hug.

"It's a bummer," she said.

We laughed at her ridiculous understatement.

"Profound summary, if I've ever heard it," I said. "And maybe all there is to say."

The kitchen restored to order, I pulled out the towel rack and hung the damp towel I was holding and told Willa I was ready to crash in the casita.

"Thanks for a wonderful dinner," I said, giving her another hug. "And thank Ed for filling the car and taking it through the car wash. Tom always did that for me. Suddenly, having it done seems the greatest luxury."

"You're welcome, from both of us. He was anxious for you to get here so he could do it."

"That is so sweet. Treat him nice when he gets home," I said, walking toward the front door. "I'd better get settled."

"Wait," Willa said. "Should I ask Andrew, or Andrew and his wife, whichever the case may be, to dinner tomorrow night?"

"If you want to."

⌒

Willa called out here just now to say Andrew is coming. Alone. He's been divorced for two years.

"Are you sure you're okay with this? Because I can call him back and say I changed my mind."

"It's okay."

"See you tomorrow, then," she said. "Whenever you want to show up at the door is fine."

I thought coming here would be an intrusion on what I've come to think of as a unique and precious time with the Lord; instead I think it might be a respite in my solitary journey. Willa makes me happy. I'm surprised I agreed to see Andrew, but it seems right. Not comfortable, but right. I'm trying to listen, trying to discern and act on the right thing. When did that begin again? I'm not sure, but I know when the impulse ceased: the afternoon we stood by a grave and told Tom good-bye.

Unpacking in the casita this evening, I was sad to realize I had all the drawer and closet space to myself. But it both surprised and pleased me that thinking of Tom was equal parts sorrow and joy.

September 9

By eleven, Willa and I had put a load of clothes in the washer and another load in the dryer and left the house with an agenda: the cleaners, the bank, and a light lunch. We had my closet full of clean clothes and dinner prepared by four, and I came out here to read and rest and get ready for the evening with Willa, Ed, and Andrew. I stood in front of the bathroom mirror putting on makeup, glad Andrew had seen me at my father's funeral and at my worst, I'd guess. Despite how kind the years are to any of us, time and gravity do their appointed work.

"Who's this?" Kelsie had asked, holding the wedding picture Katy handed her.

"Your nana," I said, looking over her shoulder. "A long time ago."

She glanced at me and then at the picture several times before she gave it to me to put back up on the shelf.

"I like you now," she said.

The girl in that picture was a stranger, and Kelsie wasn't interested in her. Others are, I've noticed. When I was home a few years ago and returning a bedspread for Mom, I ran into a friend at Penney's.

"Audrey," he had said. "Is that you?"

I wondered how the man knew me.

"It's Tim. Tim Cook."

"Timmy?" I asked. He had been my biology partner and had made dissecting a frog more traumatic than it needed to be. While we exchanged biographical information accumulated since high school, he kept staring at me. Finally he put his hands on my shoulders and looked into my face.

"What are you *doing*?" I asked.

"I'm looking for the girl," he said.

Taken off guard by such a statement, I laughed. Then I mumbled something about needing to get home.

He meant no harm, but I really have no desire to be around people looking for "the girl." It devalues the woman.

I'm glad Andrew saw me at Dad's funeral and has a mental image of me more recent than our tenth reunion. Of course, serious changes occur between forty-seven and fifty-five. If Tom were alive and by my side, I might not worry about it. But I'll walk in alone tonight, so I've thought about what I'll wear—black crop pants, a soft white T-shirt, and a beige jean jacket—and I've spent time on my hair and applied my makeup as carefully as possible, blushing my way to good health. The woman will look as good as possible tonight.

And she will give of herself. At least she'll try.

When I opened the front door, Andrew was standing in profile across the room, and I was shocked that I could easily recognize him. Tom would have called him a "flat belly," the term his golfer friends over fifty used for the thirty-something men who sometimes joined them. I've lost weight since Tom died because of a disinterest in food, but Andrew, appearing to have zero body fat, is ridiculously trim for a man his age. One does not look like that at fifty-five. He wore a cotton print shirt, stonewashed slacks, and loafers without socks. His brown hair had only a trace of gray, just enough to testify he does not color his hair. He most definitely looks like a man who would choose Clairol for Men should the need arise.

The door clicked as I shut it behind me, and he turned to look at me. The eyes are always recognizable, are they not? His were full of recognition and energy and delight. If I could have moved, I might have walked right back out the door.

He didn't come closer, and I admired the intuition that kept him across the room, saying simply, "Hello, Audrey."

Words out of his mouth, natural and pleasant, allowed me to move.

I walked into the room and smiled at two of my oldest friends standing there together, Willa and Andrew.

"You look beautiful," he said.

"You always say that."

"It's always true."

Willa had dinner on the table, except for the salmon Ed was bringing in from the grill, and we sat at the informal table in the room open to the kitchen and ate well and talked easily. The three of them seemed to sense I did not want to discuss anything personal. But when Willa insisted I repeat and elaborate on details of my trip for Ed and Andrew, I was willing, even glad, to contribute at least that much.

"I still can't believe I am taking such a trip," I said, concluding the major events that had transpired in the last month.

"You never did anything halfway," Andrew said, admiration in his eyes.

He picked up the conversation then, providing answers to all our questions. He was married to Susan only five years. They divorced two years after the reunion. At that point, thirty years old, he had decided he had no desire to be governor of Oklahoma or any other state and joined a prestigious Phoenix firm.

"Prestigious, huh?" I asked. But the question was not a reprimand, and he seemed to know it when I flashed him a genuine smile. He actually laughed, acknowledging his pretentious tendencies.

Two years later he met and married Marlene, and they had a daughter, his only child, who is a junior in college. When he mentioned his daughter, Allie, I was strangely pleased that he pulled out his billfold to show me her graduation picture, and it seemed to make him happy when I touched the face in the picture and said, "Now, *that's* beautiful."

"Her mother and I divorced after she graduated and left for college, something we had planned for some time."

"I'm sure your daughter hated that," I said.

"She did. But she seems fine with it now. She's very busy. She gets home every month or two and manages a night with each of us, a week on long breaks. It's working out."

When I asked him about work, he said he was a corporate lawyer, ready not to work so hard. He had been thinking of semi-retiring to a lake in Oklahoma and working from there when something interesting came along.

"That sounds like something people only dream about," I said.

"Do I look like a dreamer to you?" he asked.

"Well, let's put it this way—I can't quite see you retiring to a lake in Oklahoma. But what do I know about it, really?"

I got up then to help Willa bring over dessert, and Ed and Andrew talked real estate investments. Andrew and his best friend, Dan, a realtor who sold him his first house when he moved to the valley, have invested in a variety of properties together. I placed Andrew's carrot cake in front of him, thinking he could probably buy an Oklahoma lake, even if he didn't build a house on it and settle down there.

"Thanks," he said.

"You're welcome."

The ordinary and civil exchange seemed bizarre.

We talked a while longer, cleaned up the kitchen together, and considered playing a game of cards, but then by some sort of mutual consent, we decided to make it an early evening. The four of us stood in the living area near the entry, and he thanked Willa and Ed for dinner and said he had had a great time. "I can't imagine a better one, in fact."

Then he turned to me as though no one else were in the room. "I don't think you could know how good it is to see you," he said.

"It's good to see you too, Andrew."

If there was more to say, we did not say it.

seventeen

September 10

I enjoyed attending church with people I know and going out to eat with Willa and Ed afterward at a nice restaurant. I ate most of a small loaf of bread before my entrée was placed in front of me. Since my appetite has returned, I have enjoyed nothing more than carbs. If dieting becomes a necessity someday, I'll have to find a diet that does not eliminate them. (It's probably called a balanced diet.)

Willa and Ed dropped me off at the house and left to do a service project with their small group, organizing a food pantry, I think she said. Later, the group was going to gather for dinner at the home of one of the couples. Willa said that I could join them, but she had agreed to the project because it would give me the space she had promised. I thanked her for the invitation and also for her expectation of my preference for privacy.

"I'll let you work," I said, "while I lie out by your pool like a hedonistic bum."

"Good plan," Willa said as they backed out of the driveway.

I had been lying on the lounger an hour or so when I heard the door to the patio open and wondered what brought Willa back so soon. I put my sunglasses on top of my head, a crude but effective headband, and turned to see not Willa but Andrew standing in the afternoon sun.

"I took a chance you'd be here," he said. "Do you mind?"

I grabbed the sarong lying on the concrete beside my lounger and covered as much of the fifty-five-year-old me as possible, while Andrew, dressed in long khaki shorts, a blue polo shirt, and another pair of loafers without socks, dragged a twin lounger over, saying he'd rung the doorbell and had come on in thinking we might be out here.

I told him there was no "we" this afternoon.

He seemed happy to hear that.

"Do you think Willa would mind if I got us something to drink?" he asked, halfway to the door before I could say anything.

He made the trip into the kitchen and back out and handed me a soda. "Thanks," I said. "I really am thirsty. I shouldn't have come out until later, I imagine. Do you have swimming trunks on under those shorts?"

"No," he said, "but if it gets too hot, I can skinny-dip."

"Willa has an assortment of bathing suits inside."

"How provincial," he said, smiling like the boy who had looked back at me in our junior language arts class. "But I didn't come to swim. I came to see you. I should have risked calling, I guess."

I wasn't sure how I felt about this unscheduled visit. But if I'm honest, I'd have to say I wasn't completely sorry to look up and see Andrew there. We sat beside each other and talked about our children, summarizing in an hour or so a lifetime with them. After he went inside to refill our drinks and sat back down again, I volunteered stories about the grandkids, which he encouraged with rapt attention and laughter in all the right places. The rude zoo bear story started the collection of anecdotes. It had been prompted by his asking what I am going to do while I'm here and my answering I know only what I'm *not* going to do.

At one point we needed to cool off, and we chose to do it in the pool rather than the air-conditioned house. He took off his shoes and sat on the edge of the pool, swirling his legs in the water, and I got in close to where he sat and rested my arms on the edge of the pool, elbows out, hands clasped, chin resting on top of them. He asked me about teaching, amazed that my career had come and gone, and I asked him about being a lawyer. It sounded like his devotion to each and every Phoenix ball team and his love of skiing and golf consumed as much of his life as his continued interest in the arts or job and family.

Back in the loungers, drip-drying in the sun, we sat for

a while without saying anything. I closed my eyes, relaxing, even though my day alone had been interrupted.

"Are you awake?" Andrew asked.

"Almost," I said without opening my eyes.

"Will you let me say I'm sorry?"

I opened my eyes to see Andrew facing me, sitting on the edge of his lounger, his elbows on his knees, his hands clasped in front of him.

I closed my eyes again.

Then, with an involuntary sigh, I sat up on the edge of my lounger facing Andrew, our knees only inches apart.

"For what?" I took my sunglasses off the top of my head and put them on, though the sun was behind me.

"You might think this is crazy, but I'm not just sorry for breaking up with you, though God knows I'm sorry for that. I'm also sorry for ruining that night. It comes back to me, all the things you did to make it special, how you looked, how innocent and happy you were, and it makes me sick. I wish the memory weren't so vivid. And so unrelenting."

He took my glasses off my face, put them on the table between us, and looked into my eyes, searching not for the girl, but for me. Or so it seemed.

"I've made a good many mistakes in my life, but that was the worst."

"You were practically a child, Andrew. I don't mean that unkindly. It's a fact I acknowledged only recently actually, and you should too. You were twenty years old!"

"So were you," he said, "but *you* didn't leave me."

"Ah yes, well, I still think you should give yourself a break. Please. I already said I've forgiven you, but if saying you're sorry helps, then fine. I accept your apology."

"But it doesn't change anything, does it? We still lost a lifetime together."

I shrugged. "I've had a good life, Andrew, a life I wouldn't trade for anything. Don't waste a minute worrying about what you imagine we lost."

He flinched.

Once again I had been presumptuous, or at least insensitive, and I tried to soften my last words. "I know about wasting minutes."

"I doubt that."

"You said yourself I don't do anything halfway. When Tom died, I wanted to die. Or more precisely, I wanted our life back or nothing at all. I dwelled for fifteen months in Tennyson's 'The tender grace of a day that is dead will never come back to me,' and I began to think I might stay there forever. This trip is an attempt to leave there. It is an attempt to live. Even live well. I hope you never choose to regret 'a day that is dead.' Suddenly, I want very much for you to live well too."

"People would say I live very well," he said.

"So, the angst implied in 'losing a lifetime together' was mere drama? I hope it was."

He smiled. "You're being impossibly direct."

I smiled back. "I guess I am. What's the matter with me? And you're right. You do seem to have a great life."

"Overall." He looked at his watch. "You'll be glad to know I'm leaving," he said, standing up, taking my hands, and pulling me up too. "But I have tickets for the opera tomorrow night, and I hope you don't have plans and will want to go. If you don't say yes, I'll cancel my plans for this evening and stay until Willa and Ed come home and find me skinny-dipping in their pool, singing 'Tonight' at the top of my lungs."

"Don't mention that song," I said, though the context made me laugh.

Even without the threat, I found the opera appealing.

Later when I told Willa I was going, she said, "You're kidding!"

I read what Tom had highlighted in the ninth chapter of John after Andrew left. Jesus has healed the blind man, and now he speaks of figurative blindness, which has spiritual and eternal consequences: "I have come into this world, so that the blind will see."

I left home desperately needing to see. I have begun to feel like one who has been led out of the mouth of a cave into the mist of a coming dawn.

September 11

Eating a late breakfast in front of the television with Willa, I used the remote like a man, channel-surfing all the morning shows to watch the most interesting clips or interviews connected with the anniversary of our most recent national tragedy.

"Okay," Willa said, finally turning off the television and collecting my dishes, "go get ready. I'm treating you to a spa day!"

"What?"

"It's true. I called this morning, and miracle of miracles, we're in. Facial, manicure, pedicure. I'm sure you haven't done that on this little trip of yours. It'll be great, and you'll be oh so lovely and relaxed when you go to the opera tonight."

"No massage?"

"You want a massage?"

I laughed.

It was four by the time Willa and I finished at the salon and ate a late lunch. When we got back to the house, she said she had a book to finish and that I should go to the casita and have some time to myself until Andrew arrived. I don't know why I hesitated to come to Phoenix. Willa is fun and considerate, and the best friend anyone could have.

Tonight I wore the black dress I wore to see *South Pacific* in Dallas. It was my only choice, because Willa and I did not shop. After relaxing at the spa, I didn't want to spend any part of what was left of my afternoon pulling clothes over my head in dressing rooms. Besides, I doubt I could have found anything that does any more for me than that dress.

There was no doubt that Andrew approved. "I know," I said when he started to open his mouth, "I look beautiful."

"I was going to say *stunning.*"

"You look stunning too." Though I like casual dress as much as the rest of the world, I still appreciate seeing a man dressed in a nice suit and tie when an occasion calls for it.

He opened the car door for me, and I sank into leather significantly more luxurious than the leather covering the seats in my car. "Nice," I said when he was settled in the driver's seat. "I'm guessing you enjoy cars."

"One of my passions," he said, tapping the steering wheel. "But look," he said, opening his hand, "this is my oldest and most prized possession."

In the palm of his hand, I saw keys attached to a pewter disk with an *A* on it.

"*A* for Andrew," I said.

"The women in my life have thought it was *A* for Ackerman. But what it has been all these years is *A* for Audrey."

I looked into his eyes and saw nothing but sincerity and more emotional honesty than I would have thought him capable of.

No response seemed appropriate.

He put the keys in the ignition, started the car, and backed out of the driveway. "We don't want to be late, now, do we?" he said.

"Goodness, no," I said, smiling at the absurd.

⁓

The Masked Ball was breathtakingly moving. I felt accommodating when we walked to the car after the performance and Andrew asked if I would let him show me his house before taking me back to Willa's. He seemed so eager to show me I could hardly refuse. We talked about the opera most of the way to Scottsdale.

"The tragedy had a happy ending, don't you think?" Andrew asked.

"Not for Riccardo. Amelia's aria was amazing, though, and it is no wonder her husband relented and let her live."

"A tale of forgiveness," Andrew said, looking from the road to me. "No theme is more satisfying, is it?"

"Probably not."

Andrew turned into his drive, and I caught my first glimpse of a home that came right out of the Arizona architecture magazines lying on Willa's sofa table. He parked in the circle drive and took me into the house through an enormous glass-paned front door. He said the house itself wasn't huge, just over thirty-six hundred square feet, but I gasped when I stood in the foyer and looked into a living area with windows covering the back wall. This mass of glass provided, with the help of landscape lighting, a view of an infinity pool, surrounded by huge decorative tiles; luscious grass; an iron fence, boundary for a desert filled with a wild variety of cactuses; and finally, hills. Wondrous hills. Ultimate privacy.

"Oh my, Andrew, this really is spectacular!"

The furniture in his home was both massive and tasteful. He said he had employed a decorator but that he had personally approved everything, from the artwork to fabrics.

I couldn't imagine how he could have had time to oversee

so many details. "You have a good eye. I probably should have known that."

We confiscated a box of pictures from his closet during the tour of his house and sipped raspberry tea on his patio, looking at pictures of Allie from birth to the present. The pictures were back in the box, glasses were refilled, and the moon was shining on the perfectly still water of the pool when he began talking about his marriages. He said Susan had been a bad choice, but he thought for a long time that he and Marlene would make it.

"So why didn't you?"

"In the end, she wanted something else, I guess. Something I couldn't give her."

I looked around, incredulous. "And what is it you couldn't give her?"

"Myself, according to her. She said she needed *all* of me."

"*All* is a lot for one person to ask of another, isn't it?"

"*All* has a stipulative definition. What Marlene meant was she wanted someone who loved *only* her."

"She thought you loved someone else?"

"Someone else *too*. She knew I loved her, but she didn't believe she had my undivided attention, and she wasn't going to settle for that anymore. She is the mother of my child. We had a good life. I tried to talk her out of it for two years, but when Allie left for college, Marlene had divorce papers ready for me to sign."

"Do you keep in touch?"

"We have Allie. We have to keep in touch."

"Can't you get back together? For the sake of Allie. And twenty years of history. The years of history that long marriages accrue are underrated. It's one of the aspects of Tom's death I mourn the most."

"Marlene has been dating someone for quite some time now. She says she'll probably marry him."

"*Probably* sounds like a loaded word. Maybe she wants you to stop her."

"I told her marrying him would be pretty ironic. He'll never have all of her, because while she may love him, she'll always love me too. We both know that. She acknowledges the irony, but I doubt it will stop her."

"Maybe, but the irony could work in your favor."

"You think so?"

"I do." I looked at my watch, aghast that it was well after midnight. "I also think it's late. You'd better get me home."

"I can't believe you're here, sitting on my patio, and I *really* don't want to take you home."

I wanted to say, *Focus, Andrew, focus.*

Instead I pushed my chair back and said, "But you must. Let's go."

When we pulled into Willa's driveway, we sat in the car with the windows down, enjoying the night air that makes Phoenix a delight in the fall.

"You know," he said, "Marlene emotionally frisked me when we were dating, since I was divorced and high risk as far as she was concerned. And it was you that troubled her, not Susan. I never understood that completely, because the night I saw you at our tenth reunion, I realized you were lost to me forever. And while that understanding didn't help me go on with Susan, it did help me go on. Marlene and I were happy. Happy enough, I thought. On the other hand, I never did stop thinking of you, not altogether. I looked for you at our twentieth reunion, and our twenty-fifth. I never went to the mall when I was home that I didn't hope to run into you. And on a rare night when I was home alone, sitting on the patio, I wondered where you were and what you were doing. Marlene sensed what I finally acknowledged, at least to myself—I have always loved you."

He looked at me and rolled his eyes. "I know. That's pretty pathetic. But I do think we would have been happy together."

I smiled. "To quote Hemingway, 'Isn't it pretty to think so?' "

I've been into reality for a very long time now. I've seen fantasy destroy perfectly satisfactory realities. Surely Andrew has learned that.

"Early on I thought about you too," I said. "Unlike you, though, I resented that very much, which is why I've made some of the choices I've made. But you know what? I'm glad I'm here now. Perhaps it will enable you to banish any idealized memories of us so you can convince Marlene she has all of your heart."

"How could I do that?"

He leaned over to kiss me, and for a moment sitting with him in the comfortable space of that car, the idea of kissing him seemed both familiar and desirable. But I turned my head so that he kissed my cheek instead of my mouth. He leaned his head against mine then, and I closed my eyes and said a prayer for this man who had remained so dear to me after all.

"You should try, Andrew. Try to convince her she has the part that matters most."

I opened the car door and moved away from him. "Don't get out. I'm two steps from my door. Thank you so much for the opera and the tour of your home. I'll like thinking of you there."

He grabbed my hand and held it until I pulled it away and stepped into the night without looking back.

I wonder if Andrew could guess why I didn't let him kiss me. I might tell him someday, but tonight ambiguity seemed better than trying to explain that my turning away had very little to do with him and everything to do with Tom. I cannot keep Tom's kiss from becoming a memory someday, but for now, I can still close my eyes and feel it. I will hold on to that for as long as possible.

eighteen

September 12

Willa and I were on the road to Prescott by ten. Ed offered to drive us, but Willa wanted the wheel and told him so. "Play golf with your buddies," she said as we each finished a bowl of cereal, "and we'll be back before you've played eighteen holes and cleaned up." She leaned over and kissed him. "And cooked dinner. Tom wasn't the only one who can cook, right, sweetie?"

Willa collected bowls, rinsed them and put them in the dishwasher, and rushed us out the door. "He just might do it," she said as we clicked ourselves into seatbelts a minute later. "Now, sit back and watch the road from the passenger seat for a change."

When we pulled onto the freeway, she admitted that she half envied my journey. "Though I certainly don't envy what necessitated it," she said, reaching for my hand and squeezing it.

When we arrived at our destination without any problems, Willa whipped out her phone and reported her expertise to Ed, who had started his backswing when his phone rang.

"Oops," I said as she snapped the phone shut and grimaced.

"Oh well," she said, heading me toward a shop that looked promising. We ambled through it and every other shop we saw (she was in a shopping mood) and had items held for her in four of them before we took a lunch break.

"Okay," Willa said when we placed our order. "Help me decide what I need most. I can't haul four things into that house."

"Oh, you can too. The worst Ed will do is shake his head, trying to act exasperated."

"I know it. But even *I* think I've gone overboard. Really, help me decide."

"It's your decision to make, Willa."

"Do you like the buffalo painting?"

"Yes, and it will be perfect on your entry wall. But why in this world you don't want the two friendly buffalo calmly eating grass side by side on the hillside instead of the *fighting* buffalo, I cannot fathom. They're head to head, Willa, poised for battle!"

"The colors are better in that one, more dramatic."

"The image is disturbing."

"Oh, what's a little fight?"

"Perpetual discord will hang on your wall, for goodness' sake! But hey, you're right, the colors are good."

"You're too darn holistic sometimes."

"Get the warring buffalo, what do I care? I'm out of here tomorrow."

"Don't remind me."

"I've stayed longer than you ever thought I would. Admit it."

"I guess. But not long enough. Why do you have to leave?"

"I have an agenda of sorts. I plan to be in Yuma tomorrow night. I need to get on with my journey. Don't you think it's sort of neat?"

"Tell me you didn't just say *neat*."

"Did I say that? I meant neat-o."

"To tell you the truth, I think it's weird. What difference does it make if you stay a day or two longer and get to Yuma on Friday? Or Saturday?"

"I'm sure I don't have an answer that will satisfy you. I have loved being here, and I love you, and I'll be back, but I'm going to finish this journey first."

"So, you think the happy buffalo picture is the way to go?"

"I can see it cheering you up every morning when you come out of your bedroom looking for the coffeepot."

In the end, Willa decided to think about three of the potential purchases and bring Ed back for his opinion, but we returned to get the picture, had it wrapped, and with one last look at the feuding buffalo, maneuvered the happy buffalo out of the shop and into the back of Willa's Escalade.

On the trip home, Willa asked if I was going to keep in touch with Andrew. She had asked about my evening with him on the way up to Prescott, fast-forwarding opera details and rewinding details about his house and wives.

"So, did he make a move on you?" she asked after we had covered most of the evening in more detail than I'd ever wanted to provide.

I laughed—Willa has that effect on me. "Some people think *I'm* direct," I said.

"I'll bet he did. Give me the scoop."

"No, he didn't make a move on me."

"Nothing?"

"Nothing to speak of."

"Fine."

"Don't sulk. He tried to kiss me, okay?"

"But you didn't let him?"

"No."

"You feel nothing for Andrew?"

"I don't know what I feel for Andrew."

We rode in silence for a minute.

"Actually, that's not true. I'm feeling great affection for Andrew, and I very much want the years ahead to be the best he's ever had."

"That's nice."

"Yes, I think it is."

"So, you like my buffalo?"

"I do. They look peaceful, any rancor they've ever experienced a thing of the past. Like Andrew and me."

"I'm going to name them after you two, A and A."

I rested my head on the back of my seat and yawned. "That's a root beer," I said, blinking, trying to keep my eyes open.

"A and *W* is a root beer!"

We had a great day in Prescott.

⌇

I had told Ed and Willa good-night and was reading in the casita when I heard a knock and opened the door to see Andrew standing there.

"Are you still leaving tomorrow?" he asked.

I put my Bible on the bed, walked outside with him, closed the door behind me, and leaned against it. "Yes, I'm packed, my map is in the passenger seat, and I'm ready to head to Yuma in the morning after breakfast."

"You want company? I could get away for a few days."

"I've got company. Remember?"

When we'd talked by Willa's pool on Sunday, I had told him about my collage of Scriptures, the sheep I count.

He smiled. "I mean flesh-and-blood company."

"Spirit company is what I need now. Not only is the Spirit good company, but he's quite generous. He's brought good experiences and cool people into my life all along the way. But thanks for the offer."

He leaned his shoulder on the door and stood so close I could smell his cologne.

"If I e-mail you will you answer me?"

"Unless you make me mad," I said, smiling.

"I don't plan on that."

"Seriously, I'll answer you as long as it seems right. As much as I've enjoyed being with you, as happy as I am to be friends again, I think you should work at getting back together with Marlene."

I looked at the pewter key chain in his hand. "If you decide to try, you might give that *A* back to me since it stands for Audrey."

"Sorry, babe. I'm too attached."

I frowned.

"But maybe I can convince myself that *A* is for Acker-man," he said. "Would that satisfy you?"

I smiled.

He traced the bridge of my nose with his finger.

"So, how do I get Marlene back?" he asked. "How do I quit being ambivalent about whether I even want that? You know what I want."

"I know what you *think* you want. It seems to me you need a good dose of clarity. And the best way to get that might also help you get your wife back—pray."

He laughed.

I laughed too. "Well, I'm sorry, but I really can't think of anything that would help more."

I took his hand and led him to his car door. He looked at

me so tenderly that I went into his arms without hesitation, and we held each other for a long time, fully experiencing every sweet thing we had felt, and still feel, for each other. And then I opened the car door for him and watched while he drove away.

I went inside and put my Bible in my suitcase and pulled back the covers, quite ready for bed. "Believe the miracles," Jesus said in my reading tonight. (It appears reading Tom's Bible, specifically John, has become a habit.) I believe in miracles, but I also believe the change God brings to the human heart is the greatest miracle of all. Tonight, as I wait for the gift of sleep to come, I'll save the rocks the trouble and praise God for what he is doing in my heart.

September 13

The cereal boxes stayed in the cabinet this morning. We had a late breakfast and a big one, what Willa and I affectionately call an Oklahoma breakfast: bacon, eggs, biscuits and gravy, and juice. The upside to all those calories is the fact I didn't have to stop for lunch. I arrived in Yuma by four and reacquainted myself with dragging bags from the car to my room by myself. I can't say, however, that I'm not glad to get back to the rhythm of my trip. I have the sense that I'm where I'm supposed to be, at least for tonight.

I dreamed about Tom again last night and wonder if the anticipation of resuming my trip triggered the dream. In it I was taking a walk by myself in Willa's neighborhood, which became a street in Prescott. As I stopped to look in a shop window, I heard a beep and turned around to see Tom parallel parking his golf cart at the curb, which, because it was a dream, didn't make me laugh; in fact, it didn't seem the least bit extraordinary. That's the charm of dreams, I guess. Of good ones anyway.

"Audrey," he said, coming over to me. "I've been looking for you. I bought you a statue."

"You're kidding. What kind of statue?" I asked. "Where is it?"

"It's in here," he said, leading me to the restaurant where Willa and I had eaten lunch.

He led me through quaint dining rooms until we reached the back one and exited French doors onto a stone patio that encircled an Olympic-size infinity pool.

"Whoa," I said, thinking for just a moment we were at Andrew's house.

"It's down here," he said, taking me by the hand.

We hurried around the pool, across an expanse of patio, down steps, along a gravel pathway, and into an enormous garden. We crossed a beautiful lawn and stopped before a pedestal holding a large bronze statue.

"Do you like it?"

I gasped and tears brimmed in my eyes. "It's my brave."

He slipped his arm around my waist. "I know! I looked everywhere for it."

I woke up saying Tom's name and half expecting to see

my Indian sculpture on the table across the room. Tom really had searched for a reproduction of that statue. I'd hear him ask about Humphriss's *Appeal to the Great Spirit* whenever we went somewhere that displayed or sold western art. If he had located it, I doubt we could have afforded even a copy, but his persistent asking was a gift.

Perhaps the day is coming when gratitude will surpass grief.

Willa and I walked a lot while I was in Phoenix, and I've decided if my days don't naturally include substantial walking I will do thirty minutes on the treadmill at the hotel where I'm staying. It surprised me no end, my resolve notwithstanding, that I actually put my bags down, unpacked my tennis shoes and a T-shirt, and found the exercise room fifteen minutes after I arrived. I was the only person in the place and turned the television to HGTV, determined to walk the full thirty minutes. Determination was necessary, as treadmills are short on scenery and quite easy to abandon.

I hardly broke a sweat when I walked. Tom always said sweating was necessary for effective exercise, so I suppose I'll up the speed tomorrow. After I returned to my room, I rewarded myself by calling in a pizza and eating it while watching a movie. I found myself saying, as I picked up a piece of pizza, "This is kind of fun."

I haven't watched television much since I left the Grand Canyon. I've missed it. I hope it can be entertainment and information now rather than my anesthetizer of choice.

After the movie I wrote an e-mail to Willa and told her I

was safe in Yuma and thanked her for everything she did to make my stay in her casita such a pleasure. I wrote the kids about my new walking regimen, knowing they would be glad to hear discipline was now a blip on my screen, but I warned them that any celebration would be premature.

When I logged on, I was surprised to see a message from Rita, who had just sailed into Venice. She and John had enjoyed a gondola ride, had paid ten dollars each for the privilege of sitting at an outdoor table in St. Mark's Square and drinking a Coke, and had resisted buying an outlandishly priced mask at one of the hundreds of mask shops in the city. She mainly wrote to say, "No wonder you loved this place."

I did indeed. Standing on deck, leaning against the railing, I knew I'd never forget the view of the city as our ship sailed into port that summer afternoon. I told Tom I hated to be so predictable, but Venice couldn't help but be a contender for my favorite city. We must have taken a hundred pictures there. I'm sure we took one of every bridge in the city. We framed a picture of one of Tom's favorites. We're sitting in a gondola with our arms around each other and the Bridge of Sighs in the background.

The picture sits on a chest in our bedroom, and each time it caught my eye after Tom died, I thought how innocent we had been on that glorious sunny day in Venice when we posed in the gondola near a bridge with a name that turned out to be so appropriate. I wrote Rita a quick note telling her she shouldn't miss the Bridge of Sighs.

I was also surprised today to see an e-mail address I didn't recognize with the subject line *Opportunity*. Paul Keeter, the principal of the high school where I had taught, wrote a short but impassioned plea for me to take over the classroom of a teacher who was having a baby the first of March. He wanted me to finish the semester for her.

My reply was succinct: "How long do I have to think about it?"

That I would consider it astounds me.

I began John 11 tonight. In the first section, Mary and Martha sent word to Jesus that their brother Lazarus was sick. What struck me tonight was that they didn't say, "Lazarus is sick," but *"the one you love* is sick." There's something about their referring to him that way that sort of gets me. John referred to himself that way too. They were very sure of Jesus' love, a love more important to them than their own names. Maybe I should join their ranks: "Lord, the one you love is sad. Lord, the one you love is frightened. Lord, the one you love is confused. Lord, the one you love misses Tom so much."

"Let us go to him," Jesus said when he heard about Lazarus.

He has come to me too. And I thank him for that. I am finally able to do something besides sigh.

nineteen

September 14

Ah, San Diego.

Willa really wanted to come here with me. I told her we'd do it next year when Ed is off somewhere playing golf with his friends.

This place I had to do alone.

Tom and I had meant to come here. It was high on the list of must-do's he kept in the back of his mind. During a time when I couldn't get away from school, he had attended a conference on Coronado Island at a Victorian hotel, sprawling and gorgeous with its distinctive red roof, a *Somewhere in Time* kind of place. He said his trip would have been perfect if I had been there to walk the beach with him, our custom morning and evening when we vacationed on any beach.

One summer night on a warm, secluded stretch of beach

in Florida, we did more than walk. I should have been suspicious when he brought along our biggest and thickest beach towel. Rounding a bend on that moonless night and having seen no one for quite some time, he laid out the towel in front of a dune and said, "We're about to make a memory." He was not wrong. I seldom hear waves crashing that I don't think of it.

I heard them crash this evening. I'm a landlocked Missourian; no treadmill today. The minute I got situated in my room and looked out at the ocean, I decided I'd take my thirty-minute walk along the seashore. The experience was bittersweet, as I knew it would be, for this was the first time I'd walked a beach without my husband. But the sand was refreshing beneath my feet, and the ocean waves breaking on the shore, though a depressing image in some of the finest poems I know, had a calming effect on me. The return of the tide does not bring to me, as it did Matthew Arnold, an "eternal note of sadness" or the "turbid ebb and flow of human misery." I do hear eternity in it, but it is the sound of hope. I've become a student of John's gospel, which is brimming with hope, and I am increasingly grateful for "the tender grace of a day," finding it enough to live for.

I did have one bad moment this evening. I was walking, one minute on the wet sand, the next in water up to my ankles (Tom believed walking a straight line was impossible for me), and I noticed a man about Mark's age, walking in front of me at some distance. Just as I was feeling a kinship with the solitary figure, I heard feet slapping the packed sand behind me and a girl's voice calling out, "I'm here, babe! I'm here! Wait for me!" The man turned around, and a young woman ran past me, ponytail bobbing, and caught up with him. Until I watched them walk on together hand in hand, I didn't know that coveting words was possible: "I'm here, babe. I'm here."

I didn't feel like walking farther after that, and as though it were a prop brought in for this scene, I found a log, where I sat for some time and watched waves lapping the shore, hermit crabs skittering across the sand, and the sun disappearing beyond the horizon. As dusk turned into darkness, I thought of what Tom had said about his time in San Diego and agreed with him—it would be perfect if he were here. But mercifully that thought was overlaid with the thought that had kept me from succumbing completely to "death in life," the thought that sustains me still: "I am with you always."

I was okay then, sitting in the dark, hearing in the repetition of waves breaking and spreading on the sand before me, *"I'm here. I'm here."*

September 15

The San Diego trolley line is fabulous. I have a good mind to sit through the whole route again tomorrow, because the scenery along the way and places it stops are wonderful.

But my heart rate rose when the trolley crossed the bridge onto Coronado Island and I caught sight of the hotel Tom had told me about. I spent last night at a hotel on the ocean-front in San Diego, delaying gratification for this moment. I got off as close as possible to the Hotel del Coronado and walked around the grounds and finally made my way into the beautiful lobby. The mass of woodwork, dark and warm, set the mood for an ambiance that struck me as both extravagant and peaceful.

I had reached my destination and I loved it.

Not knowing exactly when I'd arrive in San Diego, I hadn't made a reservation, but boldness and optimism seized me, and I strode up to the registration desk and asked if there was possibly a room available for Saturday through Tuesday nights. The man behind the counter consulted his computer and said he had nothing for Saturday, but a nonsmoking queen room was available on Sunday through Tuesday nights.

"That's great," I said.

If a room had not been available, I would have requested a broom closet and a cot.

Pleased at the prospect of at least three days on the island, I returned to the trolley stop and rode to my next stop, Balboa Park. Most of the passengers, a good many of them children on this Friday afternoon, rushed off and made their way to the zoo. I'm proud to say I refrained from yelling "Suckers!" The truth is I've heard the San Diego Zoo is one of the best in the country, but I'm continuing my boycott of all zoos until one or all of the kids are with me.

Instead I headed to the IMAX Theater to watch *Deep Sea*,

which seemed expedient given the amount of time I plan to spend hugging the Pacific Ocean the next week or so.

I had no idea when I entered the rest room at the IMAX that another child would be waiting to snuggle into my heart. This little girl, five at the most, was trying to wash the remnants of some sort of sticky mess from her hands; blue cotton candy is my best guess. I say trying, because even on tiptoes she couldn't reach the water faucet. I looked at her face, the color of Willa's espresso, and asked if she needed help washing her hands.

She nodded and I turned the knobs to get warm water. I massaged her tiny palms and fingers with soap from the dispenser and then lifted her so she could put her hands under the stream of water.

"Feels good, doesn't it?" I said.

She nodded again.

"What's your name?" I asked, grabbing a paper towel and wetting it.

"Tabitha," she whispered.

"Oh, that's a nice name," I said. "Do you mind if I wash your face, Tabitha?"

She looked up at me with the wide-eyed adoration of a devoted subject before a benevolent queen, and I wiped her mouth.

After I had her spotless, I patted the top of her braided head and asked if she was with someone.

"My class," she said.

As safe as an IMAX bathroom might seem, I couldn't

believe she had been in that bathroom by herself. I took her hand and walked out into the common area in front of the theater and nearby snack area. Seeing a group of children about her age and two young women trying to corral them, I asked Tabitha if that was her group.

"Yes," she said, and we walked that way until one of the girls in charge, a teacher I guess, saw us and hurried over to retrieve her.

"She was in the bathroom washing her hands," I said, trying not to sound critical but wanting somehow to convey the need for caution.

"Thanks," the girl called over her shoulder as she rushed Tabitha over to the group, which had apparently viewed an earlier IMAX performance and was preparing to leave. They were almost to the door, one of the teachers in front of the ten or eleven children and one behind them, when Tabitha broke from the group and ran to me and threw her arms around my waist. Kneeling to her height, I hugged her thoroughly and told her to have a great day with her friends.

As I sat in the theater waiting to delve into the deep sea, I thought about the children of my trip, especially Helen, Jared, and Tabitha. Am I a magnet for them? Or are they a magnet for me? Or are we simply a gift to one another? The IMAX film was nice—I've put aquariums on my list of things to see now—but my encounter with Tabitha was nicer still.

It was late when I got back tonight, but I got out Tom's Bible and read the Lazarus story. I've been thinking about

Jesus weeping with Mary and Martha as they stood near the hillside where their brother was buried.

I wonder, did he weep with me when I stood by Tom's grave?

I like to think so.

Yet surely that moment filled him with joy as well, for long ago he proved his power over death when he stood with those he loved and called Lazarus from his grave.

I had another thought as I read. Looking back over my early entries, I do believe that sometime in July, Jesus called me from my tomb, and since then he himself has been unwrapping the graveclothes, one layer after another, setting me free.

September 16

I hate to admit it, because it's as predictable as loving Venice, but I enjoyed Sea World no end. Years ago I went to the one in Orlando with Tom and the kids, but I think that was before Shamu charmed visitors with his majestic agility, as surprising as Emmitt Smith performing so gracefully on *Dancing With the Stars.*

During the show a family was among those sharing my bleacher, the husband sitting next to me. He had left his two daughters on the front row, begging to be drenched, but the youngest children, two small boys, sat between their mom and dad and gasped through the whole program. The younger of the boys jumped on his dad's lap when the mammoth whale first came out of the water and propelled himself into the air, making a perfect arc. The boy, his eyes wide and shining, his little mouth forming a perfect O, turned to his dad and hugged him—pure overflow of pleasure.

I know this because of the pleasure that welled up in me. It's a wonder *I* didn't hug his dad.

When the show was over, the daughters came dripping up to join the rest of the family, and as all of them gathered their things to find the sea lions and otters, the dad said to me, "Who knew we'd bust a tear watching Shamu."

"No kidding," I said, glad someone capable of such a thing had sat next to me.

When I returned to the hotel, I checked my e-mail and found five messages waiting for me.

Mark and Molly both had written updates on the kids. The girls are playing soccer. I have to say I'm sorry I'm missing their first soccer season, but I'm scheduled to watch videos of their games the minute I return. "The kids are begging to see Nana," Molly wrote.

Willa's message was a question: "Are you sorry yet that you didn't ask me to come along?"

Paul Keeter said he'd like to have a substitute in place by Christmas, and he'd give me until the first of December to make a decision.

Andrew said, "How do I get over wanting to see you?"

I wrote the kids and told them about Shamu and my reservation for the Hotel del Coronado starting tomorrow, and I gave them instructions to zoom in on the girls when they recorded their games and to tell the kids I'd be home soon enough to make them a Halloween costume to wear to their harvest parties.

I wrote Paul and told him I'd let him know my answer the Monday after Thanksgiving.

I wrote Willa and said, "Very."

And finally I wrote Andrew a one-line answer to match his one-line question: "I'll take that as a compliment, not a real question."

After I ordered room service and watched a movie, I decided to end my day with a stroll along the beach. When I returned to my room, I stood at the window, looking at the reflection of the moon on the water, a beautiful ribbon of light, and whispered what will likely become my favorite prayer: "I love you, Lord."

twenty

September 17

I awoke early this Sunday morning, and before I showered and got ready for church, I walked the beach, taking my Bible with me. It was a two-birds-with-one-stone impulse, but it turned out to make all the difference to this day. I hardly passed a soul as I walked and easily found a quiet place to unfold my towel and sit cross-legged, reading awhile and then staring at the ocean.

I turned to John 12, which records the dinner Lazarus and Mary and Martha give in honor of Jesus. I felt as if I were walking into their home with him, smelling the fragrances of love that fill this place: the dinner Martha has prepared, the perfume Mary pours on his feet. I knew what was coming in the story. The cross is straight ahead, and what Mary and Martha do must be rest for his troubled heart.

Their offerings were on my mind as I packed the car and drove the short distance to church. They were still on my mind while the congregation sang and while the minister spoke. Like Mary and Martha, I am grateful for who God is and what he has done for me. What can I do to show my gratitude? I prayed in church this morning that I could find a way to refresh his heart as Mary and Martha did that long-ago day in Bethany.

I suppose that prayer, along with the sermon, accounts for what happened after church and why I didn't get to Coronado Island until after five—not at all what I had planned.

The minister spoke from Matthew 25, Jesus' parable about the sheep and the goats, or what Tom called the parable of "The Least of These." The minister said this parable defines the righteous as those who care for others. He said our kind-nesses are what identify us as children of a benevolent God, and in a refrain he used throughout his message, he reminded us of Jesus' words: "Whatever you did for one of the least of these . . . you did for me."

I sat there remembering one of Tom's kindnesses.

Running errands one Saturday morning, he saw a man by the side of the road holding a *WILL WORK TO EAT* sign. It's easy to ignore such signs and the people who hold them, justifying our actions, but this particular day, Tom pulled his car over, got out, and went over to engage the man in a conversation. The man's name was Harold, and Tom ended up buying him lunch at McDonald's. While they ate together, Tom discovered that Harold was staying at a cheap pay-by-the-week motel; that he had applied for a janitorial job at a local factory and would find out the next week whether he got it; that he had no family to speak of; that he had no food. He did have an old Plymouth Duster back at the motel, but the gas gauge was on empty, and he couldn't think of anything to do except to pull some cardboard out of a dumpster so he could make a sign, stand on the side of the road, and hope someone needed leaves removed from their gutters or their windows washed.

Tom took Harold back to his room, paid for another week's stay, brought his few clothes home for me to wash, and returned to the motel that evening with his clean clothes, gas for his car, and a sack full of groceries.

I didn't know you could love a man as much as I loved Tom that day.

When he stopped and checked on Harold the next week, he had gotten the job. Our church helped him get settled into an apartment, and he attends our church most Sundays, holding a sign on a street only a memory. Attempts to help aren't always so easy or successful, so this experience thrilled us. It felt like "pure religion."

Thinking of Tom and Harold and Mary and Martha, I didn't rush out of church this morning after the benediction, even with the island waiting for me. I hung around to speak to the minister.

"I'm in San Diego for only a few days," I said, "and what I'm inquiring about may seem strange. Well, actually, it *is* strange."

I think I rolled my eyes at that point, or something of that nature. He stood patiently listening when I'm sure he wanted to get home and recover from the morning's exertion. Our minister gets to church at four on Sunday mornings.

"I wonder," I said, trying to hurry, "if you know of a need I could meet today."

The minute those words were out of my mouth, I could hear Willa saying, *Tell me you didn't say that!*

I wish I could, Willa. I really wish I could.

The minister smiled, and I knew what he was thinking: Here in my vestibule stands a human greeting card.

"I have the day free," I explained, "and I just thought somebody or someplace might need a little help, maybe a homeless shelter or something. What can I say? Your 'least of these' sermon convicted me."

He looked stumped. He said he couldn't think of a thing for me to do, not that very day anyway.

I was determined.

"Is your church involved with a homeless shelter?"

"The ladies provide clothes and food for one of them several times a year."

"Do you know where it is?"

"You know, I don't. I can point you in the general direction, though."

I must have looked stricken.

"I'm kidding," he said.

He asked me to follow him to his office, where he looked up the address and gave me directions.

"Thanks so much," I said, leaving his office with the address and a resolve that seemed to come from nowhere. Maybe I didn't want to go to Coronado Island empty-handed.

I drove past the shelter twice. The storefront and surrounding area did not look welcoming; it didn't even look safe.

I wondered if there were a nicer homeless shelter to bless today.

When I walked tentatively through the front door, I found myself in a hallway with dirty tiles, a couple of them broken. It had probably already been a busy day. I peered into the doorway on my right and saw an empty chapel. I heard voices in a room across the hall and stepped in to see a large dining room with three or four people eating a spaghetti dinner at various tables. There was a counter at the back of the room, open to a kitchen beyond, where a man and two ladies appeared to be cleaning up after the lunch meal. I looked at my watch and realized I had arrived too late to help serve any hungry people.

The man in the kitchen turned and saw me standing near the doorway.

"May I help you?" he asked, walking toward me. Apparently, he didn't mistake me for someone late to lunch. He held out his hand. "I'm Bill, assistant director of the shelter."

I went through the spiel I had given the minister and was met with much the same reaction. And why wouldn't I be? I wasn't following anything close to a normal channel for volunteering. I'm not sure people appreciate or know what to do with spur of the moment.

"Well," he said, "we've got the kitchen covered. Why don't you visit with those who are finishing up and bring in their dishes when they're through."

"Then maybe I could clean the tables," I offered.

He smiled and returned to the kitchen, leaving me to "visit."

There were only three people left by then. An old gentleman and a woman of undetermined age, sitting across and down from each other, had started up something that resembled a conversation, so I approached the remaining man, who sat sullenly at a back table. His hair was pulled back into a greasy ponytail; he did not have a beard, but he had a start on one; he had on a flannel shirt, though it might have been eighty degrees outside and the air-conditioning in the shelter was poor or nonexistent; and he had not washed his hands for some time, certainly not before lunch.

What to say? How's your Sunday going?

"Lunch looks good," I said.

Dear God, send some useful words.

The scruffy man looked up from his plate, wondering, I'm sure, what he had done to deserve this intrusion on his meal.

"Do you want anything else?" I asked.

"Now, that's a fine question."

I'm an idiot.

"I mean, anything else to eat. A roll? Or more spaghetti? Another brownie?"

"No."

"Did you go to church here this morning?"

"Am I eating?"

"Trying to," I said, smiling.

He didn't smile back. A stab at humor and subtle self-deprecation had gotten me nowhere.

"I'm sorry," I said. "I'm probably bothering you. I'm just looking for a way to help."

He laughed.

Here stands a hilarious greeting card.

"What's your name?" I asked, sitting down instead of running to the kitchen.

"Jenkins."

"I'm Audrey. I live in Missouri."

Finally I said something that got his attention.

"One of my kids lives in Missouri."

"You have kids?"

"Something wrong with that?"

"Well, no, of course not. Do you ever see them?"

"Sure, lady. I fly to Missouri once a month, and every Christmas I invite them here to the shelter."

I needed a minute to think.

"I can't even call them," he continued. "Takes money, you know. I can't remember when they last heard from me."

He was finished with his plate. He wiped his mouth on his shirt sleeve and stared at me.

"Do you want me to take your plate?" I asked.

"Sure, you do that."

I stood up and reached for it and then sat back down. I opened my purse, took out my billfold, and slipped two twenty-dollar bills out of it.

"Maybe you can call your kids with this," I said.

He stared at the money in my hand and then grabbed it. "Sure. That's real nice of you," he said, shoving the bills into his pocket and heading for the door.

"Wait," I said. "Actually, you can use my cell phone."

I was digging it out of my purse when Jenkins left, slamming the door on his way out.

Bill came up to me and asked what had happened.

"He wasn't a very happy man," I said.

"No, Jenkins isn't a happy man."

"I gave him some money to call his kids."

"Oh, Audrey, we don't give out money like that. You mustn't do that again."

"Why?"

"Jenkins won't use that money to call his kids. We have donated calling cards they can use here. It's very likely he won't use your money for anything good."

I should have known that. Well, great, I had come into the shelter and violated their rules in less than thirty minutes.

"I'm sorry. I only wanted to help and it looks like I made a mess of things. Is there something I can do that might really help before I slink off into the sunset?"

"Well," he said, "there's a bathroom that needs cleaning.

Someone threw up in there, and nobody has had time to get to it."

Oops, I thought, *I don't do vomit.*

"The supplies you'll need are in a closet in the kitchen."

Someone came in from the hall and said they needed Bill upstairs, and I headed for the kitchen even though every atom in me wanted very much to head to my car. The two women I had seen earlier were scrubbing pots. I thought about asking if they wanted me to finish them up while they attended to the bathroom, but I had loused up one assignment and intended to do this one right before retreating to my Solara and Coronado Island.

That, despite the fact that the few times my children threw up and didn't make it to the bathroom, Tom took care of it. The one time he was asleep and I had no choice but to clean up the mess, I threw up myself during the whole disgusting process.

"Sorry, Mom," Molly had said. "I tried to make it."

"No problem, honey." I gagged, handing her a cold cloth. "Go back to bed."

Now I was at it again.

Armed with a bucket, Spic and Span, toilet cleaner, rubber gloves, a roll of paper towels, and a mop, I opened the door to the offensive men's bathroom. It was big enough for only a toilet, a sink, and over the sink, a mirror with a crack running like a graph catty-corner across the lower half.

I think I yelled when I opened the door. I also think I

heard the women in the kitchen laugh. I doubt they could help themselves.

I took one look at the toilet stool and the floor and ran back into the kitchen.

"Do you guys have a pancake turner?"

The women looked at each other before one of them opened a drawer and rustled up one for me.

That pancake turner saved me more time and trouble than they'd ever know. After sticking toilet paper up my nostrils, I started scraping gunk into the trash can. My eyes watered and I gagged, but I didn't throw up. I didn't need any more trouble.

After I got the stuff up (and believe me, every surface had been violated), I began scrubbing everything in sight: the toilet, the sink, the floors, the mirror, the light fixture, even the walls. I put a new roll of toilet paper on the back of the tank, since there was no holder, and went into the kitchen and asked the ladies where I might find a can of air freshener. They exchanged an amused look before one of them explained the shelter didn't stock air fresheners.

Undaunted, I found a convenience store nearby (ignoring completely my recently developed aversion to convenience stores) and bought every can of freshener they had (that would be two). I came back, held up the cans for the ladies finishing up in the kitchen to see, and sprayed the scent of lilacs in every crevice of that bathroom. Then, for a finale, I left the cans on the tank beside the roll of toilet paper in hopes that they would continue their freshening work. Backing out of the tiny space, I felt like saying, *Da dum!* I'm sure the ladies in the kitchen fully expected it.

Bill had finally returned. I noticed this when I backed into him.

"Whew," he said. "I think you've found your calling. It actually smells good in there."

"Does it smell like the fragrance of love?"

He had not been privy to my Bible reading and subsequent thoughts early this morning. "More like lilacs," he said with a smile.

"You're right, it does smell good. Now let me get out of here while my tally of good and evil is even."

"Thanks for caring, Audrey."

"Thank *you* for caring, Bill." I took out my checkbook and wrote a check that should equal the cost of my stay at the Hotel del Coronado and handed it to him. "You have a lot of needs."

"Yes, we do. So thanks for this too," he said, holding up the check before folding it and tucking it into his shirt pocket.

The afternoon was spent before I drove over the bridge to Coronado Island, but after I was checked in and settled, I walked the beach at dusk. I breathed in the ocean air, an air freshener I wish I could have left in the shelter bathroom. Fresh ocean air helped. When I came in, I e-mailed the kids and told them I'd arrived at Tom's island. I did not mention my ineptness at the homeless shelter. I'd save that for another day.

I stood at my window later looking at the stretch of beach I had just walked. "I'm here, Tom," I said. "It's as lovely as you said it was."

When I could leave the view, I walked over to put ice in my glass and pour a much-needed Diet Coke. I sat in my very nice chair and put my feet up on the edge of the bed. I was still feeling pretty stupid. My attempt to help couldn't have been more bumbling. Or humbling.

"I wasted my first day on the island, Lord," my spirit grumbled. "I didn't help. Not one bit."

I heard a response, inaudible but real nonetheless, and quite sweet: *You did it unto me.*

I smiled then, a smile that would not go away.

twenty-one

September 18

I felt fine when I awoke this morning, despite yesterday's fiasco. In fact, I felt sociable enough and brave enough to experiment with eating by myself in public. I stepped inside a casual dining room at the hotel to see if a table for one was available. I gave the packed room a cursory look and started back out the door when a lady at a table for two near the entrance jumped up.

"Ma'am," she said, "you can have this table. My husband had to run up to our room before we take our walk, but we're through." She waved someone over to clean the table. "I'll just wait for him in the lobby," she said, looking on the floor around her chair for her bag.

"Please," I said, "stay and wait for your husband."

She put her bag in her lap, told me her name was Liz Emerson, and recommended the buttermilk pancakes.

"I'm glad to hear that. I'm hungry for pancakes, despite the fact that the nutrition gurus say I'll be hungry for something else in an hour. Oatmeal would keep me until noon, but it isn't worth it."

I told her my name then, and she said that she and her husband live in Phoenix, Arizona, and spend a week on Coronado Island every fall.

"This is my first visit, but my husband has been here before," I said.

She started to say something in response but saw her husband in the doorway. "Ah," she said, "here's Vernon now."

"Feel better?" she asked when he came over and stood beside our table.

"Who'd you give my seat to?" he asked gruffly, his smile indicating he was no curmudgeon.

"I gave it to Audrey Eaton," Liz said, clearly familiar with this persona, "and you haven't answered my question."

"I feel fine," he said, offering me his hand. "Good morning, Audrey."

I told them to enjoy their walk, and they left as the waiter brought my breakfast, which was delicious, though my suspicion proved correct: Room service is much more comfortable for me than sitting alone in a dining room. Of course, I had to admit I wouldn't have met Liz and Vernon Emerson if I hadn't left the comfort and security of my room.

I passed them on the beach a little later.

"You weren't gone long," I said as the three of us stood soaking up the morning sun.

"I'm a party pooper," Vernon said. "I've got a little indigestion this morning."

"He should have had the pancakes, instead of sausage and fried eggs," Liz said, taking his arm. "Or oatmeal."

I grimaced. "Heartburn sounds better," I said. "Well, I'd better get on with my walk and see if the Travel Channel exaggerated when it named this beach one of the best in the world."

An hour later, walking into the back entrance of the lobby, I saw an ambulance in the front drive with its lights flashing, a crowd standing back from a gurney being pushed through the front doors. Liz stood by one of the emergency personnel. Before I could compute what this meant and get over to her, she had walked out behind the gurney and was climbing into the back of the ambulance with her husband.

Ordinarily I would simply have gone to my room or back out on the beach to say a prayer for this sweet couple, but today I felt very strongly that I should go to the hospital, and for once, I didn't consider sloughing off what might be the urging of the Spirit. After the ambulance pulled away, I told the manager on duty I was a friend of the Emersons and asked if he knew where they were taking Vernon. I was relieved when he picked up the phone, made a call, and told me the name of the hospital and how to get there.

I didn't find the hospital as easily as I would have liked. Of course, considering there were only right turns on the map the clerk drew me, I probably shouldn't have made a left-hand turn when I was halfway there. By the time I found Liz in the waiting room of the cardiac intensive-care unit, she must have been there alone for an hour. When she looked up and saw me, she burst out crying.

I rushed over to the couch where she sat, put an arm around her, and patted her shoulder. "I saw the ambulance pulling away when I came in from my walk, and I was afraid you were here alone. Do you want company? Is there anything I can do for you?"

"I wish you could go in there and find out what's going on. I haven't seen anyone yet, and honestly, I'm going crazy."

"Well, Vernon must be hanging in there if no one has come out yet."

Liz squeezed my hand. "Thank you for coming, Audrey. I can't believe you did. My daughter is driving in from Phoenix, but she can't possibly get here before late this afternoon. My son says he's coming, but he lives in Seattle, and I told him he should wait until we know more before he flies down. It's nice to have you here."

A doctor came into the room then, looking at the groups of people clustered together in different areas.

"Mrs. Emerson?" he asked.

"Here," Liz said, standing. I stood beside her, and we listened to him explain that Vernon had had a relatively minor heart attack but that he needed quadruple bypass surgery immediately. Liz began to shake, and the doctor and I each took an arm and guided her back to her chair. I sat beside her, and he knelt in front of her, sandwiching her hands between his.

"He made it here, Mrs. Emerson. That's a good thing, and he's stabilized—that's good too. We believe he will make a complete recovery. We can't promise that, of course, but that is what we anticipate. You and your daughter should try not to worry."

"This is my friend," she said. "My children will be here soon."

He told her she could see Vernon for a minute before they moved him to the operating room.

She turned to me before she followed the doctor to see Vernon. "Can you wait?"

"Sure," I said.

I wasn't going anywhere. I had decided this was a divine appointment.

When Liz came back from seeing Vernon, she seemed less upset, and we stepped into a courtyard so she could call her daughter and son with an update. Both of them were already en route, which seemed to relieve her. Before she hung up with each of them, she said, "Pray for your dad."

After taking care of her two children, she made a call to her sister, who began a chain of calls. "Tell everyone to pray for Vernon," she said before disconnecting.

We sat on the stone bench after she slid her cell phone into a pocket of her jacket.

"I've been praying for Vernon," I said, "and you too."

"I appreciate that so much," she said, patting my hand.

For the most part, we alternated between sitting in the waiting room and walking the corridors. After a couple of hours, we broke up the routine by making a trip to the cafeteria for some caffeine, coffee for Liz and a Diet Coke for me, and we drank it on a patio, swapping stories about Vernon and Tom. I did not plan on mentioning Tom's heart attack—what could be less appropriate? But conversation took us there, and she probed until I told her about finding him that dreadful morning.

"Audrey!" Liz said. "I'm so sorry!"

"I am too. But Vernon's getting help in time, and that makes me happy."

"I guess you know," she said, standing up and throwing her cup in the trash. "I don't know how I would have made it through this day if you hadn't been here. How can I ever thank you?"

"Being here has been my privilege and pleasure, and thanking me couldn't be less necessary."

"But I thank you anyway."

I stayed with Liz until her daughter arrived and Vernon was out of surgery. Few things have cheered my heart more than seeing Vernon's surgeon come striding through the door with a smile on his face. How happy I was that it was not time for Liz to stand by her husband's graveside.

Arriving back at the hotel, I still had time to take a walk. I grabbed Tom's Bible and found a place to watch the sunset, wondering if Tom had stopped near there to watch the sun in the same setting. The anniversary card marked the section of John called "Palm Sunday." When Jesus rode into Jerusalem on a young donkey, the people who had heard about his raising Lazarus from the dead greeted him with palm branches, symbols of victory, and called out, "Blessed is he who comes in the name of the Lord!"

As I thought about the relief that flooded Liz's face when the doctor told her the surgery had gone well that afternoon, I looked up to see the orange sun, huge and iridescent, hanging over the horizon.

"Wait a minute," I said. I got up and scurried about collecting palm branches I had seen strewn along the beach, making a mound of them.

"There," I said when I had finished.

I sat beside my altar of palm branches and watched the sun drop from sight, streaking the sky with glorious pinks and the deep purple of royalty.

September 19

San Juan Capistrano isn't far from San Diego, so I spent my afternoon visiting the mission there. The swallows and the song about them are the sole reason for this day trip. How can I possibly remember the song "When the Swallows Come Back to Capistrano"? Was it on *Your Hit Parade* when I was a little girl and Mom rolled my hair in front of the television set? Pat Boone had a version. I suppose that's the one I remember.

People call it the jewel of the California missions. I was sick to hear that it was once a huge church with seven domes and that an earthquake had destroyed most of it only a few years after it was completed in the 1700s. And as it turns out, the birds haven't come in huge numbers to build their mud nests in the ruins of this wonderful stone church for a long time, since the early 1900s, according to a lady at the mission.

But though it isn't what it was, I found this place peaceful and enchanting. I loved the remaining walls with bougainvillea draping them, the wall of bells, the fountain, the chapel. I was sitting on a low wall enjoying the fountain when I observed a little bird flitting about and wondered if he was one of the swallows that had flown over from Argentina last spring. They still come to this area of Southern California, created to do so it seems, and a few nests appear now and then among these ruins. Whether I saw a swallow or not, I'm glad the romantic notion of the returning swallows brought me to this place.

I have come to understand that tender graces remain for those who can see. The Mission San Juan Capistrano is one. And I'm happy to say I saw it.

On the way back to the island, I pulled into a large shopping area to pick up something to eat. Rather than driving to the restaurant, I turned, with no premeditation whatsoever, into a parking space at one of my favorite bookstores. It seems like years since I've spent time in a bookstore, and I found myself walking down row after row of books, pulling out one here and there, and spending even more time perusing books on display tables. I picked up several, drawn by their quirky titles, and read the backs, thinking I might buy one. But in the end, I wasn't in the mood for cute, witty, or satirical.

I did, however, leave with a book. Why it got my attention, I can't say. It certainly didn't have an interesting cover, though plain and brown is as inviting to me as anything else these days. If I'm going to attempt reading again, books other than my Bible, that is, I thought this Pulitzer Prize–winning book might be a good one to start with. I was drawn to the simple title: *Acts of Faith*. I almost put it down when I read on the back cover that it was set in the Sudan—one recent and horrific example of a fallen world. And besides that, by today's standards, it was a tome (any book that has to list major and minor characters, along with a brief description of each, is a little intimidating). But something kept it in my hand. If it's too much once I open it beyond the first pages and actually start reading seriously, I know Molly will be glad to have it, and my purchase won't have been in vain. I might even start it tomorrow, which could cut my television viewing to practically nothing.

What have I done?

twenty-two

September 20

I made a quick stop by the hospital on my way out of town, to check on Vernon and to give Liz my e-mail address for updates, and have arrived safely in Santa Barbara. After getting situated, I opened my laptop and found a message from Willa. She wrote to tell me about a series of *Oprah* programs dedicated to a cross-country trip Oprah took with her best friend, Gayle. Willa said they were "seeing the USA in a Chevrolet," beginning in L.A. and ending in New York. She ended her message by saying that Oprah had the good sense to take her best friend with her when she took a road trip. As a closure, she wrote, "Repent!" She didn't even sign her name.

I wrote back and said I would wager there were times

on Oprah's trip across the country when either she or Gayle had been the ones repenting.

Solitude has its merits.

As does fellowship, of course, and once again, I promised Willa a trip to a destination of her choice in the next year or two.

Mainly I wrote to thank her for her sweet gift. I found it yesterday, tucked in the front zipper of my shoe bag. She had taped a note on the plastic cover that said as soon as I was ready to listen to music, she wanted me to hear song ten on this Selah CD. She said she had been drawn to the CD because of its title: *Bless the Broken Road*.

"How perfect is that?" she wrote. She said she brought it home and listened to it and decided to give it to me because of song ten. "If anything sounds like you, this song is it."

After I packed the car this morning, I put the disk into my CD player. Just before I pulled onto Highway 1, I found track ten and played and replayed "The Faithful One" for at least thirty minutes, pulling over once to reach into the glove compartment for tissues. How well Willa knows me! I love the song. Tom and I had our song. I believe that this will be my song without him and that this was the perfect day for it to come to me: "With feet unsure I still keep pressing on, for I am guided by the faithful one."

I reread her note when I got to the hotel today and had to laugh at a PS I had overlooked earlier: "Please note that someone named Eaton co-wrote the song. Is that not a sign you will love it?!"

I'm going to watch *Dancing With the Stars* and then turn off the television and read another chapter of my novel. I read the eight-page introduction and reviewed the cast of characters after dinner this evening. I'll say this: It is not light reading.

September 21

I saw him first at the top of Santa Cruz Island.

I had read about the Channel Islands in my hotel room, but that doesn't adequately explain why I actually took the boat to Santa Cruz. I could have stayed in Santa Barbara and perused quaint shops, or visited galleries, or enjoyed another botanical garden. I haven't done any of those things for a while now, but instead I chose to do something I have never done. I almost regretted my decision on the hour boat ride to the island. While everyone else was buying coffee and hot chocolate and doughnuts, I was discreetly inquiring about a barf bag. That, by the way, is exactly what I called it. A more proper name for it eludes me even now. The girl behind the counter found me a Ziploc bag, and I headed for the deck at the back of the boat, where the fresh air, despite the chill and the wind, relieved my nausea enough that I could stuff the unused bag in my pocket for the return trip.

I couldn't have been happier to see shore.

As soon as I got off the boat and the other passengers scattered, leaving me alone on the pebbled beach, I looked up at the "mountain" I intended to climb and congratulated myself on a good decision. Before I boarded the boat this morning, and after weeks of needing one, I broke down and bought a backpack for this particular adventure; my trusty canvas bag could not cut exploring a deserted island. And the island really did seem deserted. I couldn't imagine how everyone could have completely disappeared five minutes after disembarking. I slipped my arms into the straps of my backpack and began walking to a path that I assumed would lead to a trail.

My assumption was correct, and I did pretty well on the trail, though several times I thought how much easier the climb would've been if Tom had been there to take my hand and pull me up when the trail was steep and footholds too sparse. Instead I used my hands to pull myself up, like a kid climbing a rock wall, only I was a tad more horizontal. I was thankful I didn't have my canvas bag slung over my shoulder. It wasn't a horrible trail, but it wasn't all that easy either, especially for a wimpy woman climbing alone. I broke a nail, which I ignored though I had a file in my backpack, and I was forced to sit and rest a few times, but I was determined to get to the summit. This was my Mount Everest. When I finally reached the top, I considered doing a victory dance with my fists in the air like Rocky. I squelched the impulse when I saw a rather handsome man striding toward me, apparently heading back down the trail from which I had come.

"You made it," he said.

I slid the backpack off my shoulders. "To the top, anyway."

"The view is worth your trouble."

"That's good to know," I said, lifting what looked like a piece of straw out of his shiny brown hair and handing it to him.

"Thanks," he said.

That's it. That was the exchange.

The impact he made on me had nothing to do with words. It was the recognition in his eyes, and I believe he saw the same thing in mine. I've experienced such recognition seldom in my life, but each time it has startled me. It happened first with Andrew and then with Tom. The third time it happened Mark and Molly were teenagers. I attended a conference for language arts teachers and experienced this phenomenon with the keynote speaker, an educational consultant and motivational speaker from the Denver area. After all these years, I have not forgotten chatting with a group of friends, getting up from the couch to throw away a cup, and seeing him across the room, engaged in a serious conversation with a woman but looking straight at me. Nor will I forget his obvious interest in and approval of what he saw. That evening he sat with the teachers from my school at dinner, and I hoped no one noticed how lively our discussion was, how easily I made him laugh, how much we enjoyed spending an evening of our lives together. I can't even remember his name now and I never saw him again, but I have not forgotten the shock of being seen.

That brief moment on top of Santa Cruz Island shocked me in the same way.

But I dismissed it and continued my exploration, trekking from one side of the plateau to the other, looking out at an ocean sparkling in the noon sunshine. I was thankful for the sun, because even with long jeans and a hooded Santa Barbara sweatshirt, it was cool. I looked down at the water far below and saw movement, which turned out to be three whales dipping in and out of the water. I felt like Wordsworth, surprised by joy, as I gasped and turned as if to tell Tom what I had seen. When I looked toward the whales again, I saw only their tails, signaling their return to deep water. *Oh well,* I thought, *Tom would have missed them anyway.*

I had an agenda for the top of the mountain. After seeing what I could see, I planned to eat the snacks I'd brought while I read a section of John 13. I found a large, flat rock that overlooked the ocean and sat down to soak up the sun and munch on granola bars, a banana, and an apple. Pulling Tom's Bible out of my backpack, I read about Jesus kneeling before his disciples to wash their feet. This simple act must have taught them so much about what it meant to be his. The first verse said Jesus wanted to show them "the full extent of his love." Loving and giving and serving seem to be synonymous. I was so blessed to be married to a man who understood what Jesus was saying in this passage.

I stood up, put my trash in the Ziploc bag I had conveniently crammed into my pocket, stuffed it into my backpack, and chugged a bottle of water. *It's happened,* I thought as I looked across miles of sea. *Gratitude has surpassed grief.*

Coming down the mountain, which was slightly easier than going up the thing, I passed a young couple and a group of college kids, but when I reached the road at the bottom and walked past an old uninhabited farmhouse, I ran into no one until I saw him sitting at a picnic table, a laptop open in front of him.

"You made it down too," he said.

"I did," I said, walking toward him, stopping beside the stone table. "And you were right, the view was worth it."

I will never be able to account for what happened next. I took off my backpack, set it on the table, and sat down. "I saw three whales."

He smiled at me over his laptop.

As quickly as I had sat down, I stood up again.

"Will you watch my backpack for a minute?" I asked, walking in the direction of two nearby sheds.

"Where are you going?"

"To the facilities," I said, pointing at the glorified outhouses.

"You don't want to do that," he said.

"I know it."

When I returned, gagging, he had put away his computer and was sitting on the table, looking across the island at a hill I didn't climb.

"What'd I tell you?" he said when I sat on the other end of the table, using the stone seat as a footstool.

"That was a very bad experience. But at least no one had thrown up in there, as far as I could tell."

"Do you always look on the bright side?"

"Actually, it's a disgusting story you don't want to hear, I assure you."

"Well, forget any repulsive latrine encounters and think about your whales instead. I was up there two hours, and I didn't see anything but miles of sky and an unruffled ocean." He held out his hand, "I'm Zack, by the way. Zack Landers."

"I'm Audrey," I said, shaking his extended hand. "Audrey Eaton." I slipped my hand out of his and nodded at his laptop case. "Is this your office?"

"It is, in a way. My job right now is to finish a book, and I can do that here, there, or just about anywhere."

"How nice."

His answer produced more questions, but I was distracted by noise on the beach and turned to see the source of it. "Oh look," I said, pointing toward the water. "Those people are kaya-king. See? Over there. That looks like so much fun to me."

"You want to kayak?"

He stood up, picked up his things and my backpack and put them in a large water-resistant duffel bag, and started walking toward the beach, where a man was dragging a kayak to shore, pulling it up beside two others.

"I rented a kayak," he explained as we walked, "but all they had left was a two-person one, which is bound to work better with two people in it, don't you think?"

I think I laughed.

He left the duffel bag with the guide, who had just rowed to shore, ready to relax, and handed me a life jacket out of the kayak sitting on the rocks beside us. This was my first experience at the sport, though I'd canoed with Tom a few times when we were first married. Mainly I had sat in the back sunning while Tom paddled. When I tried to help, I tended to head us toward one bank of the river or the other, and Tom would holler over his shoulder, "Don't row!"

Apparently I had been healed of faulty oar handling; in fact, I seemed to be a natural at kayaking, which occurred to me even before Zack said it. I know people who kayak at home. No oceans there, but lakes and rivers abound. I'm adding this to my new interest list.

We barely made it back in time to catch the last boat of the day. Zack said it wouldn't have been a disaster if we had missed it.

twenty-three

September 22

I saw him at the top of Santa Cruz Island. He looked wonderful. The gray that had sprinkled his sandy hair had disappeared, as had the lines around his eyes, which were more green than brown today. As I think about it, he looked exactly like he did the first time I saw him, standing outside my classroom so long ago, only he had on jeans and my favorite cocoa-colored sweater.

"Hey," I said, "what are you doing up here?"

He just smiled, a response that satisfied me completely. I assumed the role of tour guide and took him all over the plateau.

"Wait until you see this," I said, grasping his hand and leading him to the area where I had seen the whales. When we got close, I held my breath, hoping the three whales would make an appearance for him. I could not believe what we saw when we looked over the edge to the water far below: hundreds of whales—some barely visible, blowing water high into the air; some gliding through the water; some flying in arcs above the water like Shamu; and some diving, their tail fins waving at us. The ocean was full of them.

"Well," I said, "what do you think?"

"I think it's amazing."

He let go of my hand and moved closer to the edge, so close my fingertips tingled with fear.

"Tom, get back here."

"There are a bunch of little guys playing really close to shore. Come look."

"No, Tom, you're going to fall. I mean it, get away from there."

He looked back at me patiently and sweetly. "Don't be afraid, Audrey. I'm fine."

The phone awakened me. It must have rung three or four times before I became oriented enough to pick up and mumble a hello.

"I'm hoping I can change your mind," he said.

"Who is this?"

"Your kayaking partner."

"Oh."

He didn't say anything then. Really, what do you say to such a response?

"I'm sorry," I said, gathering my wits. "I was asleep. I

guess all that exercise yesterday did me in." I yawned and stretched. "I'm almost awake now."

"I enjoyed yesterday. And I wanted to catch you before you left your room to see if I could talk you into a field trip today. I'll come by and get you if you're up for it."

"The zoo?" I asked, my voice tinged with something between hesitancy and dread.

"I told you. It's not just a zoo. It's a garden overlooking the sea. I think you'll like it. Honest."

"I won't be ready before one."

"That's fine. I'll get some work done and meet you in your lobby at one, then."

Oh my goodness, I thought as I threw back the covers to begin my day, *are you really going to do this?*

At least I have all morning to dawdle. I need it; yesterday was exhausting. But it was exhilarating too. I loved everything about that island.

⌒

I took a break to shower and order something to eat. I still had an hour before I would meet Zack in the lobby. I hadn't expected to have company again so soon. But Zackary Landers was nice, and he was interesting. On the boat ride back to Santa Barbara yesterday he told me that three years ago he had retired as the CEO of a company based in St. Louis in order to teach in the economics and business schools at the University of Missouri at Columbia, and that he was on sabbatical this semester to finish a textbook on business ethics.

I really couldn't believe I had met someone on the top of Santa Cruz Island who lived only three or four hours from me. I told him I lived in Springfield and had retired from teaching high school English three years ago.

"That's interesting, don't you think?" he said. "You stopped teaching three years ago, and I started."

"My husband and I both retired to travel and spend time with the grandkids."

"But he died, I'm assuming."

"Yes."

"Your wedding ring is beautiful, and it's on your right hand."

"I moved it there, quite reluctantly, a month ago. Doing so was one of the miseries of going on without him. Tom died nearly a year and a half ago."

"You can see where your ring used to be," he said, touching my finger. "It sounds like you quit teaching because of your husband. I *started* teaching because of my wife."

The boat had reached the dock then, and people around us were gathering their things. He handed me my backpack, put his duffel bag on his shoulder, and we exited the boat with the crowd, saying nothing until we had walked to the parking lot and he had opened my car door for me.

"If it's okay, I'll call you," he said.

"You're *not* wearing a wedding ring," I said. "I'm assuming that means you're no longer married. If that's the case, you can call me." I told him where I was staying. "Room 508," I said. "I think you have a story to finish."

September 23

I'm leaving for Monterey this afternoon. Zack made me a reservation at an inn he thinks I will love. When he got the sabbatical to write his textbook, he decided to do it on the West Coast, where he could enjoy the scenery and spend a few weeks and several weekends with his son, Jason, who lives somewhere between Monterey and San Francisco, close enough to commute to San Francisco. Zack made plans to spend this weekend with his son, daughter-in-law, and twin seven-year-old grandsons and probably left before I got up this morning.

"So," I said yesterday, when he told me about the boys, "what are their names?"

"Kit and Carson," he said.

Names to rival Cotton and Wheat Fields, it seemed to me. The choice of names was absurd enough to elicit a raised eyebrow from me, my version of a mouth falling open.

"Really?" I asked.

"No, *not* really. I just wanted to see your reaction," he said. "One of them *is* named Carson, but his brother's name is Cade."

"Cade and Carson. Cute names."

"Jason and Carley didn't move out here from St. Louis

until his mom died three years ago. Maggie doted on the boys. They say they still remember her. Pictures of her holding the boys or hugging them cover a substantial part of their bulletin board. I hope they'll always remember how much she loved them. She worked hard to make that happen. She wrote each of them a little book of stories and poems featuring Cade, Carson, or both of them, and in another section of their books, she wrote her prayers for them. I didn't get my priorities straight until her illness, or more precisely, until her illness turned out to be terminal. She, on the other hand, always had her priorities straight."

"So did my husband. Our granddaughters, age six now, remember Tom very well, but I'm not sure about the boys. They were barely three when he died. That is another one of the miseries. I'm thankful, I really am, that the children were grown before Tom died, but I can't seem to get over wishing he had lived to help me 'teach their children after them.' He had so much to give them. I've never thought I could possibly be enough. How can we ever make up for what they've lost?"

"I'm sorry," he said. He picked up a napkin and dabbed at a tear that had spilled onto my cheek. "I meant to dazzle you with this view, not bring up something to make you cry."

We had stopped to relax and drink a Coke on a beautiful knoll overlooking a cactus garden and innumerable palm trees, and through the foliage, a view of the ocean on our left and right. He had been right. The Santa Barbara Zoo is as much garden as zoo.

"The view *is* dazzling," I said. "I'm okay. I think this is probably the first time I've said those things out loud. I assure you my children won't listen to talk of my inadequacies. Talking about loss probably made you sad too."

"We're a pair, all right," he said, standing and helping me to my feet. "What animal shall we find to cheer you up?"

"Anything. Except a bear."

Our dinner conversation did not make us sad. We sat on the patio of one of his favorite restaurants and watched the sun set on the ocean while we waited for our food. For me, ambiance doesn't get better.

While the remnants of the sun painted banks of clouds a cotton candy pink and gulls darted for scraps, I told him about my journey, including enough details about what necessitated it that he could appreciate my buying *Acts of Faith* a few days ago. "Mainly what I've done, though, is read the cast of characters four times."

"Keep working at it," he said. "It's a good book. Some of those characters will irritate you at times, as characters are prone to do, but the book is interesting and thought provoking."

"You've read it, then?"

"I have," he said. "I've been reading on this break as much as I've been writing. I just finished Charles Frazier's *Thirteen Moons*."

"His name sounds familiar."

"You might have seen *Cold Mountain*. He wrote that."

"Yes, I did see it, but I read it first. I love historical fiction. I almost majored in history."

"Historical fiction and biography are what I turn to most for recreational reading. *Thirteen Moons* is told from the point of view of a ninety-year-old man looking back on his life. The story features the Cherokee Nation, and since I'm one-sixteenth Cherokee, I enjoyed that aspect of it. You might want to read it, but be warned, it's another doomed love story. Needlessly doomed, if you ask me."

"Then I'll skip it for now. I'm certainly not up for that. I bawled at the end of *Cold Mountain*. I put down the book and stumbled into my bathroom, barely able to see, and washed my face with cold water. I finally ended up lying on the couch with a cool cloth plastered on my swollen eyes. The ending really was too horrible."

"Good thing Ada had Ruby to keep her company, huh?"

"Well, yes, on the positive side. That had to help. But I hope my little journey ends better than Inman's. The whole point of making it is to live. Dying, I could have done at home. I was doing a good imitation of it, in fact."

"Frazier isn't writing your story. Someone else is. I predict you'll make it."

"That's the first thing you said to me, you know: 'You made it!' "

⌒

I finished John 13 this morning. It'll give me something to ponder on my drive today. Jesus told his disciples he was giving them a new commandment: "As I have loved you, so you must love one another." Tall order it seems to me, loving as he loved. Yet I find myself giving it a try. And I believe it's making a difference.

I gave Zack my e-mail address when he asked for it. That was nice of me.

My in-box is seldom empty anymore.

twenty-four

September 24

The inn, my room especially, couldn't be more pleasant, and I'm sure I never would have thought to choose it; the number of lodgings and restaurants in the Monterey Peninsula seems infinite. I found a small church to attend and spent the rest of the day shopping on Cannery Row and visiting the Monterey Bay Aquarium. I wasn't prepared for such an enormous facility. I sat mesmerized, gazing at a twenty-eight-foot-high aquarium encasing a kelp forest. Except for the fact that I couldn't feed peas to colorful little fish, sitting there was about as good as snorkeling. Better, since I didn't have to do my hair again.

When I got back to the inn, I did my reading. Since my soul isn't so shriveled anymore, I read quite a bit. Chapter 14 begins with such comforting words. "Do not let your hearts be troubled." Jesus tells us how that is possible: "Trust God; trust also in me." Jesus also says here that he is the only way to the Father, which is offensive to those who embrace pluralism or prefer to chart their own course. But I do trust him, and I feel very much that I am following him to the Father. My lifetime road trip!

⌐⌐

I had six messages waiting for me when I checked my e-mail tonight, a shock to my system. But I found I was glad to get them all and didn't mind answering any of them.

Katy said she and Mark had bought a dog for the kids, and though they had paid a good deal of money for it, the cute pup, unbeknownst to them and the breeder, had mange. To make matters much worse, after a day or two of cuddling him, so did they. But once they got a nasty pink lotion from the pharmacist and covered their bodies with it twice, and after they had washed everything that could be stuffed into a washer, the unfortunate incident was behind them. The puppy loved them, and except when he howled in his cage at night, they loved the puppy.

Molly reported that on the way to preschool last Friday, little Hank had said their car smelled like chicken and toots. Jada scowled at him across the backseat and said he was so gross. "You don't know what you're missing by not taking the kids to school," Molly said.

I wrote them back and gave them a summary of my little adventures at Santa Cruz Island, the Santa Barbara Zoo, and the Monterey Bay Aquarium, where I had bought stuffed otters for the girls and penguins for the boys. "I'm enjoying these days," I wrote, "finding in them what I've been calling 'tender graces.' But speaking of 'tender graces,' " I added, "I need a grandkid fix. I'm longing to feel their sweet arms around me."

Liz e-mailed from her daughter's laptop and said Vernon was home and as ornery as ever. "Despite the scar down the middle of his chest, he's feeling better than before the operation." I thanked her for the update and said I hoped to check on Vernon myself the next time I was in the Phoenix area.

Willa wrote and said the buffalo wanted her to say hello. I wrote back and said wasn't she glad she had bought the civil pair, who have time and an inclination for pleasantries?

Andrew wrote that Marlene had gone out to lunch with him today. "She's agreed to come to dinner at the house next Friday night when Allie is home. I told her about your visit and what you said about the importance of the history she and I share. She seemed to find that interesting. I just thought you'd like to know."

"I'm thrilled to know," I wrote. "In case you haven't gotten the hang of it yet, I'll pray for your evening together."

The last message was from Zack. "I'm planning on picking you up at one tomorrow unless you write back and tell me not to come."

"Are you almost done with that book, or what?" I replied. "I love the inn, I've had a wonderful Sunday, and I'll see you at one tomorrow."

September 25

"I stopped by Rent-A-Roadster and picked this up for our drive," he said as we approached a two-seat Mercedes in the parking lot. "You're going to see this coast in style."

I had heard of the 17-Mile Drive, and it was beautiful, but so was everything else we saw, and viewing it all from the convertible was nicer than seeing it from my car—a sunroof just can't compare. Instead of going to a nice restaurant for dinner after a day driving over a good percentage of Highway 1, we stopped at a deli and put together a picnic and found a spot on the beach to spread out the blanket Zack had thought to bring. It might have been the best meal I've had on this trip.

After we had eaten and put everything away except the bottles left in the six-pack of Coke, we weren't in a big hurry to leave the deserted beach. Cars zooming by in the distance and a tanker on the ocean far on the horizon reminded us we weren't alone on the planet. But it seemed as though we were, and perhaps for this reason, Zack took me to the place in his heart he said he could seldom bear to visit, the last weeks with his wife, Maggie.

"Actually," he began, "the last two months were bad. Maggie's sister and Carley and the boys stayed with her while Jason and I were at work. Eventually, though, I'd come home after hours of meetings and wonder what in the world I was doing. By the last month, I'd go into the office very early and leave before lunch so that I could spend as much time with her as possible.

"She loved me despite my inattentiveness to her during much of our marriage, and lying beside her on those afternoons, my choices began to make me sick. I think we took two real vacations the whole time Jason was growing up. We even had to cancel our twenty-fifth-anniversary trip to Hawaii because of an emergency at work. It really was a crisis, and the company pulled out of it, but the trip was never rescheduled. A few weeks before she died, she said she hoped when she was gone that I'd do more with my life than run a company."

Zack, using a stick he'd picked up on our trek through the sand, dug trenches next to our blanket as he talked. Part of me wanted to say, *Why don't we drive through Pebble Beach again?* But part of me thought this was another one of those divine appointments, and my job was to listen.

He tossed away the stick and turned his attention to the tanker, which wasn't making much headway on the horizon. "I told her," he continued, "that would be pretty ironic. And pointless. She said it might be ironic, but not pointless, not for me anyway. She said she wanted me to get much more out of life, that she had wanted that for a long time. Maggie was filled with hope and peace as she prepared to leave this world, things she must have cultivated for years while I worked ten hours a day, sometimes six days a week.

"I quit my job in June, a week before she died. I told her I had agreed to teach business courses at MU in Columbia the next fall. 'I hope you don't mind leaving St. Louis,' I said. She said she didn't mind at all."

His wife's saying, "I don't mind at all," when she knew she wouldn't leave that bed did it for me. I grabbed my sweatshirt off the blanket between us and wiped away the tears streaming down my face. Zack smiled at me, tears brimming in his soft brown eyes, and took a deep breath, determined, it seemed, to finish this story.

"I was lying beside her when the time came for her to go."

Ah, I thought, *a tender grace.*

" 'I'm sorry,' I told her, which could, and did, apply to so many things. She put her fingers to my lips to quiet me, and then she closed her eyes and gently slipped away."

I handed him my sweatshirt, and we sat for a long while, handing it back and forth. It wasn't as helpful as a box of tissues, but it sufficed.

"We *are* a pair," I finally said.

~

He's driving back down tomorrow, same time, to take me kayaking again. He said Monterey Bay is an even better place for it than Santa Cruz Island. He's also making me a reservation at a hotel in downtown San Francisco for Wednesday and Thursday nights. I think he's enjoying showing me the area.

I told him I had thought at one point that I might go all the way up the coast to Seattle, but I've decided to go no farther north. Seattle and Portland and Yellowstone can all wait for another day.

"Good choice," he said. "Anyway, you couldn't go all the way to Seattle without ferrying over to Victoria, you know."

"That sounds lovely. But another time. I'm ready, eager even, to head east. Although I'm considering taking a slight detour to see southern Wyoming."

Zack had spent unprecedented time with his grandsons in the last several months, so he understood my sudden and overwhelming desire to get back to my family.

"There's no danger of home becoming a tomb again?" he asked.

"I hesitate to sound so confident, but I'm sure it won't. It might be a refuge, as home should be, but not a tomb. I'm a mountain climber now, a mule rider, not a zombie."

"Yes, you are."

"I sat down this morning and mapped out the rest of the trip. I'm hoping to get to the end of John by the time I get home. When I let Tom's Bible ride along with me, I had no idea how much it would affect this journey of mine."

"Your husband would have known, I'll bet."

"Yes, and I *should* have."

"How's *Acts of Faith* coming?"

"Slow. Did you know that book has no stopping places? Chapters are often too long to work. It's the only book I remember reading that required me to bookmark at a paragraph. I'm still working on it, though. But it's John I'm committed to. Many things are contributing to my healing, but nothing more than that."

Zack had pulled into the driveway of the inn to let me out before returning the roadster. "I'm sure you need to get on with it," he said, "but I don't look forward to your leaving."

I turned to him and smiled. "Isn't that something?"

I read from John 14 when I got back to the room. "I will not leave you as orphans," Jesus told his disciples, and he promised to give them the Counselor, the Spirit that would abide with his disciples forever. He had come, and his followers experienced peace beyond understanding. I've had such a sense of the Spirit's presence in my life during these weeks on the road, and I think it is he who is leading me toward home.

Gratitude is welling up again: Thank you, thank you, thank you!

September 26

We paddled through the kelp forest along Cannery Row. The exercise was invigorating, the scenery was beautiful, and the critters were delightful. We saw otters everywhere. I would never have done this alone. That's what I told Zack while we ate an early dinner together.

"I can't thank you enough for giving me the opportunity to explore Monterey Bay in a kayak."

"It was my pleasure. You looked like you were having fun."

"I had a blast, but I'm feeling guilty about your book."

"Don't worry about my book—it's right on schedule. You and I haven't gone anywhere before one in the afternoon, and I'm an early riser."

"My husband was an early riser. I've always thought rising before seven to be primitive. On school days, I had to get up at six, and in thirty years of teaching I never made friends with that hour of the day, never stopped groaning when the alarm went off. I think that's why I like sunsets so much—it's the only time I'm awake to see the sun do its thing with the horizon. A few weeks ago, however, I did see a spectacular sunrise over the Grand Canyon. I, and at least a hundred international travelers, loved it."

He was smiling.

"What?"

"You're funny."

"You're nice."

He reached across the table and put his hand over mine for the briefest moment. "*This* is nice." Leaning back in his chair again, he said, "Being with you is nice. I've dated a few times in the last year or so, but it just wasn't fun. I pretty much gave it up."

"I'm sorry, but I understand. I can't imagine dating."

He laughed.

"Can you imagine kayaking with a new friend?" he asked.

"Tell me that's not the same thing."

His smile and his eyes, kind and warm, make me happy.

"I went to the opera with an old friend in Phoenix two weeks ago and haven't once thought of it as a date. It was . . . what?"

"A shared experience?"

"That works."

"Well, my shared experiences haven't been fun either. And don't be sorry. Teaching has been fun, writing has been as fun as such hard work can be, taking in the world around me has been fun, having time to be with my family has been fun. That's a lot of fun, don't you think?"

"Tender graces."

"What?"

I looked across the table at him. "Tennyson's 'the tender grace of a day that is dead will never come back to me' has become for me 'the tender grace of a day.' "

"Shall I add Tennyson to my recreational reading?"

"I don't know about that, but the abbreviated line probably works for you as well as for me. The things you called fun are among the many things I have begun to see as the tender graces each day brings."

He looked at me in that intent way of his and smiled again.

"I think of you as a tender grace," I said.

⌒

Ruby and Pearl don't have an e-mail address, so when I returned to the room this evening, I wrote them a note on the hotel stationery that began, "The Lord is sending me back home to Missouri before I make it to Oregon ☺." I told them Willa and I might do the Oregon coast and Portland next summer and that I'd give them a call if that happened. I told them they had blessed my life, and I enclosed my phone number and address in case they ever want to make a trip to Missouri. And in the spirit of Willa, I added, "You would love Branson!"

I e-mailed the kids then, the message they've been waiting for: "I plan on being home about a week from now—next Tuesday or Wednesday. I'll call you Wednesday, but if you have nothing else scheduled, please plan on coming for the weekend. I want to have dinner on Saturday to celebrate both my return to the land of the living and Molly's birthday. I want soooo much to see my babies. My big kids too. I love you."

Then I sat down to read a section of John 15 about the vine metaphor. I think grasping this truth is one of the keys to living an abundant life. I think it explains where I am today. He is the vine, and we are the branches, and as long as we remain connected to him we will be healthy, capable of producing "fruit."

I am a healthy branch these days, Life and Light no longer my antithesis.

twenty-five

September 27

From my hotel room downtown I can see the ocean. San Francisco is a fascinating city, probably the most compact city in America. I wish Tom and I had come here. He would have loved it. When I arrived shortly before noon, Zack had left a message that he'd pick me up at three for a city tour unless I called. Three gave me enough dawdle time.

"Do you like the hotel?" he asked when I met him in the lobby.

"Very much."

"Are you up for a tour?"

"Don't I look like it? I haven't clicked across a hotel lobby so fast since I was in Dallas."

"That's a story, isn't it?"

"Well, not much of one. To answer your question, yes, I'm ready to see San Francisco."

He drove me down streets made famous in movies and television shows. That's one thing I liked about New York. Afterward I watched *Law and Order* with an experienced eye. "Remember seeing that, Tom?" I'd say while we ate dinner in front of the television. Now I'm eager to go home and watch television shows and movies set in San Francisco.

We abandoned the car at Fisherman's Wharf and boarded a boat for a tour that took us around Alcatraz. When we returned to land, we spent the rest of our time walking Fisherman's Wharf, perusing shops, though we had no intention of buying. "You can be glad Willa isn't with us," I said, which called for a brief explanation. I made a short story long when I told him about the buffalo pictures.

When the sun began to set, we realized we were starving and stopped to eat at a nice restaurant on the wharf.

"My son and daughter-in-law wanted me to bring you to dinner at their house," he said. "But I didn't think you'd want to do that on this particular trip. I told them maybe another time."

"Please tell Jason and Carley that I appreciate their thoughtfulness. I also appreciate your understanding. You're a sensitive man, Zack Landers."

He laughed.

"Are you thinking Maggie wouldn't believe someone would say such a thing?"

"Something like that."

"I read once that the suffering that comes from losing someone we love has the potential of making us better. The old person dies, and a new one is reborn. I think your wife would be so proud of the new you."

"I hope so. Thank you for the very nice thought."

He left the car parked at the wharf and walked me back to the hotel. One of the long streets was the equivalent of a ten percent incline on my treadmill, and he took my hand and pulled me the remaining few feet to semilevel ground. We took a few side trips to see the lobbies of several hotels near the one I'm staying in simply to marvel at the opulence.

"We're a long way from the Sudan," I said.

"Still plodding along in your book, huh?"

When we made it back to my hotel, he walked me into my lobby and over to the elevators and pushed the Up button. "The usual time tomorrow?" he asked.

"I'll be ready."

"We have one more day before you leave. I thought you might like to explore Sausalito, and I have a surprise for you tomorrow night—if you trust me enough."

The elevator door opened.

"I trust you."

⌒

In chapter 16, Jesus speaks again of going away and the Holy Spirit coming to us. Intellectually, the indwelling of the Holy Spirit is a difficult concept to get hold of. Experientially, it is simpler. He is like an ever-present

Jesus: comforting and confronting, guiding and equipping, enabling and enlightening. His presence is the greatest of gifts. I'm sure Andrew thought I was a little weird when I said the Spirit was good company. I hope someday it makes perfect sense to him when he sits on his patio and looks at the hills.

Even though I wish beyond what I can say that I could look up and see Tom sitting across the room waiting for me to finish typing so that we could go to bed, I believe that in Jesus, I have everything I need. I'm sure only someone who has tested his claims can understand that is not a paradox.

September 28

I read a chapter in my novel last night since I happened upon one of a rational length. When I turned out the light and stretched out under the cool, luxurious sheets, I realized that I am getting used to being alone in a queen-size bed.

I loved sleeping with Tom. Our wedding night was the first time I had slept with a man. I was twenty-two and quite ready to be with someone—considering that someone was Tom Eaton. In between lovemaking, amateur on my part but wonderful nonetheless, we lay there talking and laughing.

The first morning of our married life was as memorable

as the joy of our wedding night. My eyes still closed, I awakened, trying to discern what my feet were touching and finally realized it was Tom's sturdy and hairy legs. Thus began the comfort of sharing a bed. It was a comfort I cherished for thirty years, one of the things I have missed most. The very human side of me can hardly stand getting used to his not lying beside me.

I did not pray for it, because it didn't seem right, but I know I lay there wishing that the memories I had relived would cause me to dream of Tom. I was disappointed when I woke up this morning and realized he had not come to me.

I suppose that's the main reason I read some more in John this morning. I've taken over Tom's Bible. Though I still call it Tom's Bible most of the time, it's really our Bible now. Reading it helped me get ready for this day along with and better than my shower and room service brunch.

I was in decent shape by the time Zack arrived. I enjoyed the Golden Gate Bridge, Sausalito, and dinner at yet another quaint local restaurant.

"I didn't dream about Tom last night," I said after we had been led to a table in the corner of a dimly lit dining room and had placed our orders.

He just looked at me.

"I've dreamed of him often since he died, especially on this trip. I found him sitting by a river near Santa Fe, lounging in an inner tube on a lazy river ride near the rim of the Grand Canyon, and parking his golf cart on a street in

Prescott. In the last dream I had about him, he was at the top of Santa Cruz Island watching a whale extravaganza in the ocean below."

I could not believe I had introduced this topic and then proceeded to develop it. What was I thinking? Though it proved rather embarrassing, I backed up and explained why I had wanted to dream of him last night.

"I'm sorry for bringing up such a crazy thing," I said when I had sputtered through the explanation.

"Don't be," he said. "I'm glad to hear it. I understand it. And I'll tell you something just as crazy: I *did* dream about Maggie last night."

"Oh my gosh."

"That's pretty much what I thought when my alarm went off this morning. I don't dream very often at all. I can remember dreaming about Maggie only one other time since she's been gone."

"Is it a dream you can tell me about?"

"There really wasn't much to it. I was sitting on the patio reading when Maggie opened the door and came outside. She seemed surprised to find me there. She sat down, handed me her glass of tea, and asked what I was reading. The next moment a basketball court appeared in the backyard a few feet from the patio, and Jason asked us to come play H-O-R-S-E with him. She got up and headed into the house. 'You go,' she said. 'I've got something I have to do.' The last thing she said before going in was, 'Have fun.' "

"Did the dream make you happy or sad?"

"Both."

"Yes! Both. Always."

Then he changed the subject, asking me about progress on my book.

"Reading larger sections of John requires more of my time. But don't worry—I'm not abandoning the novel. My television viewing has taken a real hit, though."

Of all the joys of the day, what thrilled me most, of course, was his surprise. After dinner we parked in a crowded parking lot in a semi-residential area and walked around the block to the front of a huge old church. Most people pouring into the vestibule were dressed nicely, but some, thank goodness, came as casually dressed as we were.

"What's going on?" I asked.

He handed me a program he had confiscated from a side table. "A concert," he said.

"What kind of concert?" I asked, ignoring my program and following him down the center aisle of pews.

"If you don't like a string quartet," he said after we were seated, "you're going to be disappointed."

I grabbed his arm. "We've come to hear a string quartet?"

Had I mentioned I love stringed instruments? When I turned to ask, Zack was nodding toward the stage, where four musicians, dressed in black and carrying their instruments, were taking their seats. No time for a question. I opened my program to see what awaited us and couldn't wipe the smile off my face.

September 29

I met Zack for breakfast in the hotel at eight. I had a long drive ahead of me. I had told him at the elevators last night that I didn't expect him to do such a thing, but he reminded me that he was an early riser and a breakfast eater.

"Okay then," I said, getting into the elevator.

He came to my room after breakfast and helped me gather my things and carry them to the parking garage.

"A bellman could have done this, you know," I said as we rolled bags down the hallway.

"I wanted to do it."

I stopped in midstride and looked at him. "How can I ever thank you for all the things you've done for me in the last week?"

"You can't, so don't try," he said, smiling and starting down the hallway again. "Come on; let's get you on the road."

We arrived at my car and he arranged my luggage neatly in the trunk and slammed it shut.

"I need to find a Cracker Barrel. I might be able to rent *Acts of Faith* from its collection of audio books. Wouldn't that be a perfect two-birds-with-one-stone?"

I said this because I had no idea how to tell him good-bye. We stood beside the car, looking at each other as we had done across a number of dinner tables.

"If this were a date," he said, "I'd kiss you."

He looked like he very much wanted to do that. I reached up and put my hand on his face, rubbing my thumb slowly and gently across his lips. "But it's breakfast," I said, "and a lugging my stuff to the car."

"It's you," he said, "finishing a journey."

I managed a smile. Then I got in the car, backed up, and headed for Elko, Nevada. In my rearview mirror, I saw Zack walking toward his car. He had said at breakfast that he was glad he had a book to finish.

⌒

I wish I had stopped somewhere to fill up and get a Coke besides the beehive near the interstate. After I filled my cup of ice with part of the cold liter of Diet Coke I had bought, I was heading out of the crowded parking lot to find the ramp for I-80 when she backed into me. It was not the first time in my driving career that my car and I have heard that dreadful crunch.

"Darn!" I said.

The car that had backed into me pulled forward, and a woman, hardly more than a girl really, jumped out of her car, looked at mine, and started sobbing. I got out of my car and walked over to her.

"Hey," I said. "It's okay."

"Lady! I smashed your car!"

I heard crying from a different direction and looked into the back of her little Civic to see two car seats, one occupied by a sleeping infant and the other by a distraught toddler.

"Why don't you get your little girl?" I said.

She wiped her face with the palms of her hands, and while

she retrieved her toddler, I grabbed some tissues from my glove compartment and assessed the damage to my car.

"I can't seem to do anything right today," she said when I handed her the tissues. "My husband left for Iraq yesterday, and I'm trying to get to Sacramento to stay with my parents for a while. This is just awful," she said, nodding at my car.

I went around to check the back of her car. "You're not in too bad of shape," I said. "You've broken a taillight, but you should be at your parents' before that's a problem. Your dad can put in a taillight, I'll bet."

"Ma'am, I only have liability insurance. I don't know what to do about your car." She looked miserable, as miserable as the girl trying frantically to get into her hotel room in Texas a few weeks ago. But at least she had stopped crying, as had her daughter, whose curly little head was buried in her mother's shoulder.

"You haven't done much more than dent a fender, and I have a friend at home who fixes dents. You just take care of your babies and get to Sacramento."

She started crying again, and I dried her tears with the tissues in my hand.

"Everybody makes mistakes, honey, and you have a lot on your mind. Don't worry. Okay?"

"Okay," she said, trying to smile.

By the time we were on our way, I had learned her name, as well as her husband's, and I had told her they were going on my prayer list. I had every intention of praying Margo Greer all the way to Sacramento. She took down my address so she could thank me properly even though I insisted that wasn't necessary.

Maybe I don't wish I had stopped somewhere else, even if I do have a fender to fix.

The music filling my car from the Christian satellite radio station gave me sweet truths to celebrate, and I arrived at my destination in a good mood. Since I had told a friend good-bye, had managed to get a fender smashed, and had driven ten long hours—that's a minor miracle.

twenty-six

September 30

I was on the road by nine this morning. I woke up at seven, got ready, and checked my e-mail. There was a note from Willa, saying the buffalo couldn't imagine anyone spending the night in Elko, Nevada, and notes from Molly and Katy saying they couldn't wait until Saturday and everyone would be there by noon. There was also a note from Zack. I delayed opening it until I had answered the others.

I told Willa to tell the buffalo they shouldn't knock Elko until they had tried it, and I told the kids I was hitting the road again after a restful night in a Nevada hotel room and that I couldn't wait either.

By the time I finished three brief replies, I had delayed gratification enough. I clicked on Zack's message. "I've grown used to 'shared experiences,' " he wrote. "I looked at the clock at one yesterday and hated that you were getting close to the California border instead of waiting for me in your lobby. Be safe as you head to Wyoming."

I read his message twice, packed the car, and read it one more time before I answered him and put the laptop in the car.

"You'll be crossing the border yourself soon enough," I wrote. "Or have you forgotten you live in Missouri too? I'd like to read your book sometime."

I listened to praise music until I stopped on the other side of Salt Lake City to fill up and grab a late lunch. Then I did something rash, even in my healthy state of mind. I turned to a station that plays love songs. The interstate was so deserted as I neared Wyoming later that afternoon that I thought it had been constructed just for my return to Missouri. Driving did not require rapt attention; thus, when "Power of Love" began playing, Celine's voice took me from that interstate to any number of roads on which Tom and I had traveled with that particular song playing. I drew in my breath and blinked away the tears that threatened, and yet something kept me listening.

"I'm your lady, you are my man. . . . We're heading for something, somewhere I've never been. I'm frightened, but I'm ready to learn, the power of love."

Blinking couldn't contain the tears. These words described how Tom and I had started our life together. But fear had been discarded quickly, and the promise of the words had been realized: I learned what love between a man and woman can be. Oh yes, I have been there.

⌒

Utah was prettier than I had expected it to be, even from the interstate, but the closer I got to Rock Springs, Wyoming, the more beautiful the terrain became. Wyoming is definitely a vacation destination. A national forest nestles in the southwest corner, and mountains and rivers surround Rock Springs, where I stopped for the evening. A little daylight remained when I got there, so before I got something to eat and found a room, I roamed the area looking at the scenery. In the process I located a church to attend tomorrow morning at ten thirty. There must have been endless places to explore if Zack and his kayak had been there. I'll tell this area what I told the Grand Canyon when I was there with Tom and the kids: "I'll be back." For now, I'm in Tom's horse-heading-for-the-barn mode, though I'm pulling in the reins tomorrow. My plan is to both dawdle and worship the morning away and still make it to Cheyenne by nightfall.

Tonight I didn't even turn on the television. I seem to have lost interest in it, although I'm sure it will come in handy when I'm home and need to chill. I didn't open my novel tonight either. I had come to John 19, the death and burial of Jesus.

The account was so matter of fact, but it was full of a cast of characters affected by Jesus in his dying hour. Reading it, I wondered if those who knew him and loved him could have recognized the blood-drenched body of Jesus as he hung between heaven and earth and did his redemptive work. Yet the only words he said on the cross that alluded to his suffering were subtle and ironic. The one who brought living water to the inhabitants of this world said, "I thirst."

How can that be?

October 1

I made it to Cheyenne without a ticket, a flat tire, or a fender bender. "Woo hoo," as Willa would say.

Before I left the Rock Springs area this morning, I attended a small church. The few scattered around the room looked anesthetized. I felt sorry for the minister. Maybe I encouraged him, because I was obviously engaged. Or who knows, looking at an expectant face might have unnerved him. I'm sure I've depressed my minister many times in the last year as I sat in my pew comatose. "Awake, my soul and sing" seemed like an impossible prayer at the beginning of my journey, but it's happened. I'm awake. And I'm singing.

In fact, I continued to worship across Wyoming, listening to, and sometimes singing along with, the praise songs on the radio. I heard Phillips, Craig, and Dean's "Shine on Me," one of my favorite songs and prayers. "Breathe" is another prayer I heard. I've sung it in church many times, thinking, if anything, that it was a bit much. But in the car today, I understood it and owned it: "This is the air I breathe, your holy presence living in me. This is my daily bread, your very word spoken to me."

Then, wouldn't you know, I even heard Selah's "The Faithful One."

That started the crying.

Everything I heard today moved me. My tissue stash in the glove box was depleted, but fortunately I had snatched a handful of tissues from my hotel room and put them in the passenger seat for such a time as this. I knew I wasn't through crying. I'm glad my self-imposed silence is over; this music is healing. But I do hope by the time I hit Missouri, all these tears will have done their cathartic work.

I had messages waiting for me when I got settled in my room this evening. Molly wrote asking if everyone could come up Friday evening after the guys get off work instead of waiting until Saturday. I replied that dinner would be waiting for them at six thirty, and in honor of her birthday, an Italian cream cake would be waiting too. That will thrill her.

I was almost nervous clicking open Andrew's message but relieved to read it: "Friday night went well. I hope that makes you happy."

"Very happy," I wrote. I hoped Marlene was reading his message and my reply over his shoulder.

Finished with my messages, I turned to John 20.

The tomb is empty! (Thanks anyway, Joseph.) This chapter records appearances of the risen Lord. This has to be the ultimate contrast of emotions, ultimate healing for desolate hearts.

I can imagine being there, witnessing grief turning into astonishment and joy. I especially identify with Mary. I can imagine how frantic she was when she couldn't find the body of Jesus. I can imagine how her heart must have stopped for a moment when she heard him call her name so softly and sweetly. I can imagine her turning toward him and finding in his smile everything she had been looking for.

I don't know how Mary was able to leave Jesus that morning, except that he had asked her to deliver a message. What must she have looked like when she ran to the disciples, breathless, and said, "I have seen the Lord!"

October 2

What would Willa's buffalo have to say about Hays, Kansas? Well, I can't worry about that. Hays has a Pizza Hut, and tonight that was enough for me to call it charming. Tom would applaud my stamina on the road today.

I found a *Law and Order* and, for old time's sake, watched it while I ate my pizza.

Then I checked my e-mail. There was only one message tonight, a short one from Zack: "You're almost home. I'll be in Missouri for two weeks between Thanksgiving and Christmas, trying to get ready for the spring semester. Want to have another shared experience?"

It was a sweet message, and I sat there for a long time

trying to think of how to respond. Finally I wrote: "I'm pretty sure I do. Call me."

I'm so excited about getting home tomorrow I might have to take an Excedrin PM, or whatever PM is in there. Or better yet, I'll count my sheep one last time on this journey: "I will fear no evil, for you are with me"; "It is I, don't be afraid"; "I am with you always"; "I will never leave you nor forsake you."

Actually, what I read in John tonight gave me another group of sheep to count, the "It's the Lord" group.

Peter and several of the other disciples had gone out the night before to fish in the Sea of Galilee and caught nothing. Now Jesus stood on the shore in the early morning light and called, "Friends, haven't you any fish?" When they answered no, he told them to throw their nets on the right side of the boat. While they must have been sure doing so would prove futile, they dropped the net and found they couldn't budge it for the great number of fish.

The minute this happened, John exclaimed, "It's the Lord!"

Oh, I love that.

And I love this: When John gushed his joyous and obvious conclusion, Peter jumped into the water in order to get to Jesus! (It was going to take that boat a while, towing 153 fish—whoppers, I'll bet.)

I have some understanding of how both John and Peter felt. God has been at work on this trip. So often I have felt like exclaiming with John, "It's the Lord!"

A wise woman sitting with me by the Survivor Tree, a young policeman issuing a warning ticket, a cowboy in black rescuing me on the side of the road—it's the Lord! A little companion helping me tackle seven slides, Ruby and Pearl prying me from my room to share a meal with them, Andrew and I making peace—it's the Lord! A bathroom needing to be cleaned, Liz Emerson offering me her table, and Zack standing in the sunlight at the top of Santa Cruz Island—it's the Lord!

Can such good gifts, such tender graces, come from anywhere else?

My last encounter with Tom even seemed ordained. I don't think it was so much a matter of my showing Tom the view from the top of Santa Cruz Island as Tom and the Faithful One letting me glimpse glory.

Do you see me, Lord, thrashing through the water to get to you? Do you see me falling at your feet in gratitude and joy?

October 3

I can't believe it!

I'm home.

Mark and Molly have been here. They must have come Saturday or Sunday. The house is spotless, and they've planted pansies in the flower beds and put more of them in a huge pot on the porch. When I came into the house, the first thing that greeted me was a Welcome Home banner with a colorful finger paint border made up of the babies' handprints. What good children I have!

I carried the luggage into my bedroom, unpacked the overnight bag, and decided to leave the rest of the unpacking until tomorrow. As I looked around the room I hadn't seen for so long, the picture of Tom and me in the gondola seemed to beckon me. I walked across the room, picked up the picture frame, wiped away the dust the kids had missed, and looked at the happy couple. "I've been to Coronado Island, Tom," I said, "and it was just as lovely as you said it was." After the briefest moment, I put the picture back in its place and picked up *Acts of Faith* and also *Gilead*, another Pulitzer Prize winner I had bought just before Tom's death and never opened. Bringing them into the living room with me, I put both novels on the side table by my chair to read later and sat down to read the Bible I had laid in my chair when I first came into the house.

I turned to the end of John, a passage full of forgiveness and redemption, and read the whole last section, though Tom had not highlighted it. Jesus and Peter have a sweet encounter that ends with Jesus saying to Peter, "Follow me!" With these words, Peter's new life begins.

A passage that implies new life seems the perfect ending for John's book and my weeks on the road. I smiled when I closed Tom's Bible, realizing that tender encounters with Life and Light have graced my days. I thanked God for all that he had shown me and done for me on this journey from death to life, I thanked him for this record of it, and I thanked him for finally bringing me home.

I leaned my head against the back of my chair and closed my eyes. "Oh, Tom," I said, "I still miss you, but I'll see you in God's good time. And I'll have so much to tell you!"

Acknowledgments

I would like to thank David Kopp, an editor who encouraged me to write a novel when it seemed as unlikely as winning the Indianapolis 500 or landing a space shuttle or making a quilt. I laughed for years at his suggestion and then, as an act of faith, gave it a try. I would also like to thank Erin Healy, my freelance editor, who has taught me so much. And at Bethany House, I am grateful for David Horton, Charlene Patterson, and Rochelle Gloege—I have loved working with them.

I am most grateful for my daughters, Stacey Myers and Leanne West, and my mom, Dorothy Sublett, who enjoy books endlessly and read with joy and discernment. They have read my manuscripts the same way, always believing I have something to say and encouraging me to say it. And I'm also grateful for several friends (you know who you are) who read this manuscript and offered help and encouragement.

"Woo hoo!" as Willa would say. Or as Audrey might say: "I am blessed."

JACKINA (pronounced with a long "i" to rhyme with China) STARK recently retired from teaching English at Ozark Christian College to spend more time writing and traveling. During the twenty-eight years she taught at OCC, she traveled nationally and internationally to speak and teach, and wrote many articles for denominational magazines. She has been married to her husband, Tony, for forty-two years. They live in Carl Junction, Missouri, and have two daughters and six grandchildren.

If you enjoyed *Tender Grace,* we also recommend:

A captivating story of a broken, isolated woman and the flawed, faithful people who help her forgive and find peace.

Home Another Way by Christa Parrish

Eleven years ago one event changed Miranda DeSpain's life. Tired of living in its shadow, she decides to confront her fears. But doing this means she must find a missing, crucial piece of her past.

In Search of Eden by Linda Nichols

What happens when one woman's greatest dream means ruining another woman's only hope?

Waiting for Daybreak by Kathryn Cushman

Looking for More Good Books to Read?

You can find out what is new and exciting with previews, descriptions, and reviews by signing up for Bethany House newsletters at

www.bethanynewsletters.com

We will send you updates for as many authors or categories as you desire so you get only the information you really want.

Sign up today!